My Silver Shoes

BY THE SAME AUTHOR

BOOKS

UP THE JUNCTION
POOR COW
FREDDIE GETS MARRIED (FOR CHILDREN)
THE INCURABLE
I WANT (WITH ADRIAN HENRI)
TEAR HIS HEAD OFF HIS SHOULDERS
THE ONLY CHILD

PLAYS

STEAMING
EVERY BREATH YOU TAKE
THE LITTLE HEROINE
SISTERS

My Silver Shoes

NELL DUNN

BLOOMSBURY

First published 1996

Bloomsbury Publishing plc, 2 Soho Square, London W1V 6HB

A CIP catalogue record for this book
is available from the British Library

ISBN 0 7475 2735 0

Typeset by Hewer Text Composition Services, Edinburgh
Printed in Great Britain by Clays Ltd, St Ives plc

TO SISSY

CONTENTS

The Fall *1*
Off to the Day Centre *13*
Jonny Speaks *31*
Cleaning *37*
The Night Joy Left Big Tom Twenty Years Ago *47*
The Chiropodist *53*
The Sex Scene *69*
Jeff Speaks *79*
Gladys Speaks *85*
The Fleas *97*
Gladys Speaks Again *107*
The Holiday *117*
Jonny Comes Home *135*
Jeff Leaves *145*
Getting the Wallpaper *153*
Goodbye, Jonny *167*
The Caravan *179*

THE FALL

My name is Joy and once upon a time I knew where I was going and what I wanted. It was years since I'd divorced Big Tom and now I lived in a flat bang next door to Gladys, my mother. I liked calling her Gladys. Jonny had grown up and moved in with a girl, but they'd split and he'd joined the Army on the rebound and was stationed in Northern Ireland. I had a boyfriend called Jeff who worked in dry cleaning.

It was Monday morning and rainy out. I drove to work in my little Fiat. Brian was already waiting by the door when I got there.

'Hello, Brian, put the kettle on.'

'Hello, Joy.'

There were four new punters at the Job Club that morning and they had to be registered and fitted in. I knew what it felt like to be out of work and skint. The photocopier had packed up again and someone had stolen a sheet of stamps. Brian made the tea.

'Do the stats for me, Brian, I'm going to help Patsy with her C.V.'

Brian did the stats. He liked helping me.

The next day Jeff and I were going to Ibiza, and while I was away Peter, my locum, would be running the club.

'I'll bring back a couple of bottles of wine and we'll have a nice drink when I come home. So behave yourselves and go to your interviews and get jobs so my stats look good.'

When she got home that evening Joy gave Gladys last-minute instructions to water her plants and keep an eye on the Fiat and go in and dust round before they got back.

'I'll phone you when I get there, Mum. Be sure to be in. Is Teddy staying?'

'He's no good. I don't know what I've got him for. He used to give me a pound or sometimes a fiver. He gives me fuck all now. Here, Joy, here's a tenner to spend on yourself.'

And she thrust a note into Joy's hand, knowing she wouldn't see her in the morning because they were getting an early flight and she'd still be asleep. Then Teddy turned up.

'Hello,' said Gladys, 'coming in?'

'I've brought a hot pie,' said Teddy and they went into Gladys's flat.

Teddy, small and dilapidated, sat in his overcoat in the corner smoking a cigarette and watching the racing on telly. He didn't have a lot to say but he munched now and again at his gums while Gladys bustled about with knives and forks and clattering of plates, talking all the while.

* * *

Joy stayed up late ironing her clothes and packing and unpacking again, to see if she could fit in one more dress.

'Fuck me,' said Jeff, back from his evening deliveries, 'I thought we were only going for a week.'

Early the next morning they flew to Ibiza.

The first day Joy sunbathed topless on the balcony and burnt her tits. Jeff rubbed baby oil into them for hours but she wouldn't let him touch her anywhere else.

'Too hot,' she said.

In the evening when it was cooler they went down to the sea.

Jeff went for a long swim. Joy stood and watched the whisk of his flippers all the way to the horizon then she lay on her back in the shallow water letting the gentle waves move her body to and fro. She closed her eyes and thought about the thick cream lace she'd seen in a shop they had passed. She wanted some for new bedroom curtains and she wondered if she dared ask Jeff to buy it for her on his credit card.

Joy thought about her flat: the slatted white-wood cupboards Jeff had built in the bedroom with small china door handles decorated with rose-buds and little shelves beside the bed all painted white and on the walls pink and red roses running riot. She had chosen the paper and Jeff had hung it. Now all she needed was that thick lace to cover the glass door on to her balcony and perhaps hang in swags over the window? No, maybe swags would be overdoing it. The carpet was white wool, and she was still paying for it, but she loved the feel of it between her toes. Now Jeff had moved in he was paying half the bills and it wasn't so bad.

She wondered if she had been right to move next door to Gladys. They'd had a birthday party in the spring. Gladys was eighty. It hadn't turned out well. Gladys had accused Joy of trying to steal her limelight by dancing the jitterbug with Jeff and Jonny got drunk and told his grandmother she was too old to have a boyfriend and when Gladys had shouted it was none of his business he'd hit Teddy and knocked him down.

Jonny had apologised the next day and neither Gladys nor Ted had mentioned it again but the thought of it got on Joy's nerves and Jeff wasn't above mentioning it when he wanted to have a go at her.

Now Jonny was stationed in Northern Ireland and didn't get home much. It had surprised the life out of her when he'd walked in one day and said, 'Mum, I've joined the Army.' 'What!' she'd said. 'You always tell me I can't do nothing without you. Well, I've joined the Army.' 'Good luck, darling,' she'd said and kissed him, scared out of her wits that he'd screw everything up by shooting his gun in the wrong direction or losing his uniform. Anyway, it was too late to think of that now. He'd passed his medical. He was a soldier.

She didn't want to think about Jonny any longer because she was on holiday and Jonny was a worry to her. Ever since he'd split up with Jackie he'd had these depressions. She knew in her bones the Army wasn't right for him. He was a strapping young man on the outside, but on the inside?

The sea lapped cool against her neck and she tried hard to imagine how the cream-lace curtains would blow back and forth in her bedroom window as she lay in bed with Jeff and all would be well with Jonny and the Army.

Then Jeff was beside her.

'Had enough?'

'Enough of what?'

And smiling he pulled her out of the sea and they shook out their towels and dried themselves and went and had a drink in a beach bar and after a couple of Campari and sodas Joy mentioned the lace.

'We'll see,' said Jeff.

The next day she kept her T-shirt on. Jeff hired a jeep and they drank beer in a little bar by the sea. Then back in the car he turned off the road and they bounced down a track between poplar trees and got lost.

Joy sat on the bonnet smoking a fag. They got out the camera and took lots of photos and she posed this way and that. Then he lifted her off and carried her over to where he'd stretched out his jacket under an olive tree and dropping to his knees he laid her down.

When they got back to the apartment she was exhausted and fell asleep on the bed.

Jeff woke me at midnight. He said, 'Come on, we're going out,' so we went.

I was sitting at the table in the restaurant thinking about the sex we'd had under the tree and I got turned on.

'You watch me pull that waiter,' and he said, 'You dare,' and I said, 'You watch.'

I got up.

'Could you show me where the toilet is, please?'

And he led me up the stairs and I stood talking to him at the top where I knew Jeff could see my ankles and feet and nothing else. I was wearing these high patent sandals, shiny and red. When I came out Jeff was standing just outside.

'We're going back to the apartment right now!'

Next night we went to this German bar and I was jiving with the Guvnor and everybody was watching and clapping.

When I came back to our seats Jeff was chatting to a Chinese woman and buying her drinks. He was loving every minute of it. I felt left out. Jeff looked good. It was turning me on and I gave him a look and went back to the Guvnor. Jeff went on buying her Pernods. He knew I could see him.

Now I'm singing on the mike and Jeff beckons me over. I can see he can't get rid of this Chinese Lady.

When I got over there she said to me out of the blue, 'I don't like you.'

'And I don't like you, neither,' I said.

Jeff said, 'We've got to go.'

'No, you wanted her, you have her.'

'No, I want you, not her.'

'We'll go home when I'm ready.'

When we got home I undressed. He watched me. I felt like a glamour girl. We were awake the rest of the night.

The next day they bought the lace for the curtains and a lace bed-cover to match. Joy saw some tiny pearl crosses. They turned out to be a set: a necklace and earrings to match. She wanted it and Jeff bought it. Then she bought him a cigarette lighter in a turquoise-leather pouch to hang around his neck.

On their last day Joy was beginning to look forward to being home and back at work and showing off her sun-tan which being blonde she knew she wasn't meant to have.

She wondered how Peter was managing (and she hoped it wasn't too well) and if he could cope with Melanie. Melanie, whose mother was a Seventh Day Adventist. Melanie, who was very bothered when James came to the Job Club in shorts and sat all afternoon with his feet on the windowsill sunning his legs. She complained to Joy that his genitals were exposed if you looked up the leg of his shorts which she could do from her desk and when Joy mentioned this politely to James he said in a very loud voice specially for Melanie's benefit, 'My doctor insists I get a cooling breeze to my private parts,' and tempers had flared and James had threatened Melanie: 'It would be down to you if I come up in a bad rash and am unable to attend an interview for work,' and Joy had calmed them both and made tea and Patsy had run to the corner for chocolate digestives and the storm was quelled till the following day when James walked in. When Joy said, 'Take a seat and wait a minute,' he shouted at her, 'Who the hell do you think you are?' 'Exactly the same as who you are, a human being,' came back Joy quick as a flash, and after that James was as good as gold and ended up teaching anyone who wanted to know how to use the computer and do spreadsheets.

* * *

In the afternoon they hired a lilo and Joy lay stretched out in her red bikini while Jeff swam behind and pushed her all the way to the lighthouse island.

And that was Joy and Jeff on holiday in Ibiza.

When they got home Mrs Bell met Joy on the walkway.

'Your mother's had a bad fall down the steps of the Wimbledon Theatre. They've taken her up the hospital.'

For a moment Joy thought she was going to be sick. She dropped the bags and ran down the concrete stairs and then ran up again screaming for Jeff who was already halfway down after her.

Jeff drove her to the hospital and there was Gladys lying on a bed in a side ward in Casualty, a bandage round her head and blood on her cheek.

'Oh Mum, whatever happened to you?'

'Where've you been, Joy? I've been looking for you.'

'I've been on holiday, Mum.'

'I don't know why they brought me here.'

'Mrs Bell said you fell down the steps of the Wimbledon Theatre. Was it on the outing to *Jack and the Beanstalk*?'

'*Jack and the Beanstalk*?' Gladys looked puzzled. 'We went somewhere on a charabanc, that much I do know. It's this fucking coat you bought, it's unlucky.'

We waited in Casualty for three hours. Jeff went home. She'd had five stitches in her head and a cracked rib.

'I'm not staying here all night,' she said.

Then they X-rayed her head but they couldn't find anything.

'Where've you bleeding been?' she said. 'I've been all on my own.'

'I've been on holiday with Jeff.'

'Why didn't you take me?'

I took her home. Her hair was all caked with blood. I got some bicarbonate of soda and washed it out. All the time my stomach was churning. She couldn't remember anything about the accident, not even *Jack and the Beanstalk*.

I slept in with her but I woke suddenly terrified.

Suppose something happens to Mum? Then suppose Jeff leaves me, and Jonny's in Northern Ireland? Suppose I have a haemorrhage in the middle of the night? What'll happen to me if I'm on my own? What'll happen to me if Mum dies?

And I lay sweating with terror and in the morning my nightdress was drenched.

After her fall Gladys was never right. She didn't want to let Joy out of her sight. And when Joy insisted she go to bed in her own flat as she Joy must go back to work in the morning Gladys slept in the chair without getting undressed.

And when Joy got back from work she was standing out on the walkway waiting for her.

'Where've you been?'

'I've been to work, Mum.'

'Couldn't you take me with you, Joy?'

She hadn't changed her clothes. She refused to cook or clean.

The social worker came and advised Joy to give up her

job and take the attendance allowance. That way they wouldn't have to put Gladys into a home.

'She could attend the Day Centre three days a week so you'd have a little break. Your mother's had a bad fall. It's affected her brain and made her confused. This is the early stages of senile dementia brought on by shock,' she said.

Joy simply couldn't believe what had happened. As to what they were going to live on, she was used to having money in her pocket. She couldn't expect Jeff to pay for everything. She'd always been to work.

But as I was living next door I thought: Buck up, Joy, she is your mother and Jonny's grown-up so you haven't any other responsibilities and it would kill her to go into a home.

So with a heavy heart I told the manager, 'Perhaps it's only temporary till she gets over the shock. Please hold the job open for me if you can.'

I gave up my job, Peter took over, and I got the attendance allowance, and, the three days she went to the Day Centre, I went cleaning. I needed the money.

OFF TO THE DAY CENTRE

The first time I took Gladys to the Day Centre I'll never forget that day as long as I live. We walked over and I went in and sat down with her. She wanted me to stay. I stayed for about fifteen minutes and then I left. I cried all the way home. I kept ringing up to see if she was all right.

The first few days she'd walk out and turn up at home.

'Fuck it, I'm not staying up there with those people.'

Slowly she got used to it. It took weeks. Then she started the painting class, brought home loads of pictures. We had to buy a cork board and pin them up in the kitchen. That pleased her. Now they pick her up on the second trip and she has a ride round Putney while they're picking everyone else up. She likes that, even now it's winter. She often gives Eddie, the driver, a tip as if she's been on a coach outing.

When she's happy her whole face glows. She came back today so full of herself.

'I beat Eddie at dominoes. He gave me a game in his lunch hour.'

When she came back today it made me happy.

'I'm so glad you enjoyed it, Mum.'

'Oh I loved it. You should come up there! Eddie would let you ride home on the bus with us.'

I take her to a special clinic once a fortnight. First we go to the dementia doctor. I know every word by heart.

'How are you?'

'Fine, thank you.'

'Are you still smoking?'

'Only a couple a day.'

'Are you still going to the Day Centre?'

'Yes, three times a week.'

They check her sugar, her blood-pressure, her heart, her ears.

She gets her feet done now. And there's a new deaf-aid coming. You should have heard her when I ordered this deaf-aid. She went mad.

'I'm not fucking deaf.'

I said, 'Why don't you just try it, and if it helps you, Mum, I'll cover your hair over so no one will see it. Then you could have a conversation with people. It's because you can't hear, you miss things.'

'I'm not fucking deaf,' she said, 'it's the way they talk.'

Monday I'm getting her eyes done. She's going to have new glasses.

So we went to Boots the chemist, and had her eyes tested

and I picked her out some nice glasses and she said, 'I don't have to pay for these,' and I said, 'Oh yes you do, Mum.' She didn't like that. Her eyes hadn't deteriorated in five years. I picked her out a lovely pair of glasses. They came to thirty-five pounds and I had them scratch-proofed.

So she said to the woman, 'Can I pay these weekly, two pounds a week?'

I could have fucking died.

'No,' I said, 'you pay for them now.'

'I can't afford them.'

'Yes you can. You've got some money saved up.'

Gladys slept on the settee last night in all her clothes and next morning she says to me, 'I've washed and dressed myself. I'm ready to go.'

'You slept in your clothes.'

'Did I? No I never.'

'Teddy told me you did. Come on, change your underclothes.'

'These are all clean. I dressed myself this morning.'

'You've got to change or you'll smell.'

'I don't stink.'

'Take your dress off and have a proper wash.'

'I've got fleas.'

'No you haven't.'

The bus arrived to fetch her and she didn't know where she was.

'I'm not ready. You'll have to come back for me.'

'I'll walk her up when she's dressed.'

'All right, love.'

And Eddie went.

Tripping on the mat, Gladys lurched to the right. I caught her.

'That heel's loose, Joy, that's what's done it.'

'You shouldn't be wearing high-heels, the nurse told you.'

'I'll do what I like. She can't tell me what to do.'

She hadn't had her pills. I'd laid them out.

'What are they for?'

We have this every day.

'The big one's for your blood sugar. This one's for your angina. This one's an aspirin to thin your blood. This one's to calm you down when you go up the wall.'

'I'm not taking those. They're stale.'

Now I'm angry and I frighten her to make her hurry up.

'You've got to take these pills for the rest of your life. Otherwise you'll die. And I don't want you wearing that old dress because you've put on weight and where you fill it out it's got shorter.'

'I don't like long dresses.'

'I can see your knickers when you sit down.'

'Mind your own business!'

'Take your pills!' I shouted.

'The blue one to make my hair grow, the big one for side-effects, the white one to calm me down and the aspirin to thin my blood.'

She popped all four pills into her mouth, took a sip of water and swallowed with a great gulp. Tears jumped out of her eyes and landed on her cheeks where they sparkled under the bright electric light.

'All in one go!'

'About time.'

'If you're like that you'll end up with nobody, like me.'

'You've got Teddy.'

'He doesn't want me. He wants that ginger woman. He doesn't even try to have sex with me – that's when you can tell. He don't even give me a packet of fags, smokes fucking mine. I hide them now. Have a look at my head, Joy. I can feel the little bastards coming out and crawling all over.' Glad bent her head as she talked. 'Mrs Rand at the Centre, she's bought herself two second-hand tellies. One has the picture and the other one talks. Only cost her a fiver each. I think I'll have a snack before I go, Joy. I'm hungry and I won't get no dinner till twelve o'clock down there.'

Joy looked to see what was in Glad's fridge. Bacon, mushrooms, tomatoes and a couple of eggs. 'A hearty eater' is what they call her at the Centre.

'Shall I make you a sandwich?'

'They're all old up there, Joy.'

'How old do you think you are then?'

'I'm nothing like them. I'm a woman of the world. I went through the war. One day I'll get myself washed and dressed and I'll go.'

See if her milk is still fresh. Smell that bit of bacon. Joy made her a tomato sandwich and Gladys tucked into it.

'I don't really like the Day Centre. It's not what I'm used to. I thought I'd have a laugh and a drink and be happy,' she said with her mouth full.

'It's a day out, Mum.'

'Day out! What are you talking about?'

'I'm going to buy a Bingo set next week for you to take up so you can be the caller.'

'They won't have that. There'll be a fucking row over that. Somebody will nick it. There's one there, she's been a lady. She talks like a lady, you can tell she's been titled but she's gone off. She doesn't half go wild. I've got another one on my table you've only got to say one little word out of place. She's a cow, she is, that's why nobody will sit with her. If you upset her you've had it. She'd wipe the floor with you so I don't mix with her.'

'Eat your sandwich, we've got to go.'

What's in this bag? She hasn't used this for years: two plastic hats and a pair of castanets from that holiday we had in Spain fifteen years ago.

'Mum, you've got to throw these out and you've burnt a hole in the new kitchen counter Jeff made for you.'

'You're too fussy.'

'No, I'm not. You've got burns in your bed-cover. I told you not to smoke in bed. You could catch yourself alight.'

'Then I'll sleep in the chair where I can have the ashtray – I've got to have a fag if I wake up. I feel stifled when I'm in bed. I can't just lie there.'

The lace curtains with the little cupids and outside, the green plastic window boxes with a pink ice plant: 'Even flowers in winter.'

'Come on, put your hat on and let's go. I've got to go to work this afternoon and clean a three-storey house.'

'The Executive?'

'Yes, the Executive, so get a move on.'

'I'll get indigestion.'

'Finish it as you go along.'

Joy put her coat on over her track suit, bustled Glad out of the door and locked up.

'Who do you go to tomorrow, Joy?'

'The Chinese lady and I have to kneel on the floor to make the futon.'

'I can't go up the road like I used to or I'd come and help you. I'm a bit frightened now going out.'

'But if you look at some of the old people you can say thank God I'm not as bad as them.'

'Oh no, I'm not as bad as them.'

'If somebody else is knitting and they drop a stitch you can pick it up for them.'

'What would I want to do that for? Those people are too set in their ways. They always sit in the same seats. Now when I used to go out with Daisy I was happy. Now she's gone the other way. She ain't the same. I go to Eve's. She's not the same.'

'They're old, Mum.'

'So it's no good going with any of them. They've got no life in them.'

Icicles hung from the concrete runnels above the dustbins, crystal-clear icicles. A cutting wind darted around the corner of the building catching Gladys full in the face and blowing off her hat.

'Fuck that hat, Joy. I'm not wearing it no more.'

But Joy didn't hear because she was chasing that hat down the ramp.

'Got it!' she shouted triumphantly to Gladys.

'I said I'm not wearing it again!'

'Come on, you'll get ear-ache!'

'I'd rather be out and about, Joy.'

'But who do you know who wants to be with you, Mum?'

'Eh?'

'They don't want to go out with you. They've got their own little lives. They sit at home and they do their work. At least you've got Teddy coming up three times a week.'

'I don't want him! Let him go! I'd rather find another bloke with a bit more life in him. Plenty of men about.'

'Not your age-group! You phoned Bert up the other day, didn't you?'

'Eh?'

'You phoned up Bert. Keep hold of my arm down these steps.'

'Oh Bert, yeah.'

'He didn't want to know.'

'No, he didn't want to know now.'

'No, Mum, because he's nearly eighty.'

'Yeah.'

'And when you're eighty you should stay indoors.'

'I don't tell 'em I'm eighty. Bert's only seventy-eight.

'Well, he's younger than you then. But he's set in his ways.'

'Of course he is, he's set in his ways now. He doesn't want to know nobody now.'

'You said to him, "We'll go out for a drink."'

'He doesn't want to go out for a drink with me. Besides, he's too old to go out with and I don't think about drink now. I like a drink but

I don't go gallivanting like I used to. I can't do it.'

'Oops, hold up! You can't walk without falling over.'

'I'd rather come with you.'

'You've always lived your life through me. Even when I was twelve and the country holiday fund paid for me to go to Wales.'

'I was a bit nervous of you going at first.'

'You came too and ended up getting off with the bloke. Do you remember, Mum, Mr White, he was called?'

'Yes, he had two dogs called Sandy and Rusty.'

'That's right, Sandy and Rusty. We had our photo taken with them. I wonder what's happened to that?'

'What's become of the Whites over the road?'

'They're dead!'

'Dead? Oh he led her a terrible life down here. Poor little cow's life was a misery. He wouldn't allow her out. She never used to speak to anybody! But she clumped him in the end. She went out. What become of Daisy Galloway?'

'She's dead. They're all gone and dead now.'

'What was his name? Billy . . . Billy somebody . . .'

'Billy Eusters.'

'Who?'

'Billy Eusters.'

'Yes. Billy Eusters . . .'

'Well, he's dead as well.'

'They've all gone? Billy Eustace, that was it! Margy still lives at 36?'

'No, Mum, that was thirty years ago.'

They're all dead. I'm the only one left. There was Jack,

Sid and Ben. They were the three boys. There were seven girls. Aggie, Ethel, Emmy, Alice, Rose, Gin and me. They had good years, they were all in their seventies and eighties when they died though they had terrible lives. They met the wrong men. My Gin, she didn't know Gratton from shit. He was a baker came round our house selling bread and cakes. He chatted her up, he had this and he had that, and my Gin fell for it. He took her round his house in Chelsea and she never came home all night. Next thing we heard she was in the family way. That was it.

'Aggie's dead, Joy. Been dead for years. Ethel's dead. I've got no one. No brothers. No sisters. Just on my own. I'm the last one.'

There was something about windy days on this estate. It was as if the wind did special conjuring tricks of whistling down a concrete walkway and sweeping up all the dust and then flying round the corner and flinging it full tilt into Gladys's face before she had time to shut her eyes. She turned her back.

'Ouch, Joy, my eye!'

Joy handed her a hanky and she dabbed and blinked to wash out what felt like a bucketful of grit. The wind bounced off the concrete wall and came back at her catching the end of her scarf and unwinding it so she nearly lost it. It was slippery and Gladys clung hard to Joy's arm.

'I looked after you, now you're looking after me.'

'You didn't look after me when Jonny was born.'

'Oh don't bring that up again.'

'I was all on my own when I started the pains. I ran out into the road and a milk float took me to hospital.'

'I was meeting George at the tea-rooms.'

'What about the day before I had him when I walked all the way up to Kensington Gardens, to see you, because I didn't feel well, and you said go home?'

'Go home? You frightened the guts out of me,' said Glad. 'I didn't want you to have the baby there. You wore a blue-and-white spotted dress and you were as big as a barrel.'

Joy shivered.

'You gave me two bob to go home with and the next day it started. I can see this milkman now: "My baby's coming!" I yelled, so he drove me down the Fulham Road on the back of his float and slung me in the hospital. Nobody was with me when I had Jonny. I was all on my own in that labour ward. They put my legs through these stirrups and the matron slapped my face. Well, I was screaming.'

'My supervisor told me at work. "Gladys," she said, "you've got a little grandson." I went on the piss and the next night I went up the hospital with the Old Man to see you.'

They'd arrived at the Centre. Joy opened the door.

'You run in, Mum, I'm going home, see you later.'

'Mind how you go. What time are you picking me up?'

'The bus is bringing you back.'

'All right, love, I'll see you later.'

Gladys went through the glass door and Joy turned up the drive. When she looked back Glad was at the window waving. She was still waving as Joy turned the corner and went out of sight.

When she got home there was a letter on the mat from Patsy.

Dear Joy,

I just wanted to write and tell you how much you have helped me at the Job Club. As you know I have been out of work for a year now following a miscarriage and a long period of depression. I felt a failure because I left work to start a family and ended up jobless and childless! When I enrolled at the Job Club I didn't know what to expect.

Joy sat down and lit a fag then she read on.

I was still depressed and unmotivated and had no confidence in my prospects of getting a job. Within ten minutes of my first day, you put me completely at ease and created an atmosphere so friendly that I was able to share my experience of depression when it came to my turn to introduce myself.

After that first day, Joy, I went home and started spring-cleaning my flat which I'd been neglecting along with myself. You were always so smartly dressed, Joy, that I began taking pride in the way I dressed again. Please come back soon, we all miss you here, and though Peter is nice, it's not the same without you . . .

Love and hugs from Patsy.

P.S. No job yet but I always think of how you told us all about what you'd been through and then I know I'll get there in the end just like you did.

P.P.S. You probably think I've taken a long time

getting around to writing to you but you know me. I hope your mother's going on OK. I miss you.

'I miss you too, Patsy,' said Joy to herself, 'and you'd never guess how much.' She went along the walkway.

Indoors at Gladys's it smelt musky, old people's smell, thought Joy, and she opened the window in the bedroom. She put the clean peach dress back in the wardrobe with a white cardigan draped over it. Joy had matched all the dresses in the wardrobe with cardigans. The green with a blue-flowered one, the beige with a brown. For every dress there was a cardigan all chosen at charity shops and boot sales. All washed and ironed and matched up and hung in the wardrobe. And as she worked she ached for her Job Club.

She mourned the early morning drive across Richmond Park, where sometimes a deer would stray on to the road and all the cars would stop to let it cross, often followed by others, and all busy drivers would feel better for it and smile to themselves and breathe more deeply. And Joy would run in, late for work, some punters already waiting at the door.

'Sorry, darling, a deer crossed the road,' and everyone knew she'd be in a good humour and the day would race by.

Now, always working alone, cleaning here or there, she missed the company, she missed the laughter, even the dramas when things got tricky, stranded as she was in this existence.

Joy pulled a wedge of hair out of the plug hole.

I've told her about this. Fag-ends are everywhere and big brown burns: on the pink counterpane, the plastic covering of the bedside table, the soap dish.

She finished tidying and went back into her own house. The telephone rang. It was Jonny. He was unhappy in Ireland.

'You've got to stick it, love.'

But she hated him being unhappy.

I'm frightened of him coming back and I'm frightened of his staying there. It ain't like if the floor's dirty I can scrub it. There's nothing I can do to help him. Sometimes he rings me up and says, 'I'm all right, Mum, don't worry about me. I love you.' But I know he's not happy. I can tell. I can sense it in his voice, something that's not right. It sounds like fear deep inside.

And Joy, echoing his fear, stood stock still by the telephone and wondered how she could protect her son from the dangerous world.

She looked out into the bright winter light. Where had autumn gone? The black trees stood stark still as if playing that game of Statues where children must freeze when the music stops.

Then Jeff turned up.

'What are you doing, Jeff?'

'I miss you, Joy. Come to bed with me.'

'What, now?'

'Yes, now.'

'I'm not even washed and dressed.'

They both laughed and Jeff leant over and kissed her eyelids.

'I'm too miserable for sex, Jeff.'

He bent down and lifted her in his arms like an old-fashioned bridegroom and carried her over the threshold of the bedroom and laid her on the bed and she cried and he comforted her as best he could, slowly and for a long time. Then he rushed back to the van to deliver the rest of the dry cleaning and got shouted at for being late but he said there was a terrible jam on Putney Bridge and anyway however much they shouted it was worth it a million zillion times over.

And Joy got herself together and went and cleaned the Executive's house.

JONNY SPEAKS

I didn't know the Army would be like this. When it's very very bad I ring Mum but she can't talk when Jeff's there. So I lie down, if I can, and think about the caravan.

It's August and warm when I wake up and she lets me get straight into my blue swimming trunks.

I put on my trunks and sneakers because I like running very fast. I run very fast to the ditch and then I turn round quick so I can see Mum watching me. Then I sit under my tree with my bread to tame the moorhens.

I can hear Nan talking. We come here with Nan. My Dad is in prison.

I hear the sea. It rumbles quietly. Mum talks to Nan.

'Poor little sod. Let him do what makes him happy,' Nan said. 'He's no trouble really.'

'Let him do what he likes,' said Mum.

I was happy doing what I liked. I watch Mum. In and out and in and out of the caravan. Teapot. Milk jug. Bread and butter. Fried eggs and bacon. I can smell the bacon from where I sit under the tree. It mixes with the tree smells. Mum is wearing a yellow blouse with little puffy sleeves and shorts. She flits in and out. In and out. The radio is on. Someone is singing, 'Cupid, draw back your bow . . .' Nan sits at the table tucking in.

'Would you like some breakfast, Jonny?' Mum calls.

'Can I have it over here?'

She comes towards me blotting out the sun. The moorhens run to the ditch. She has curls, blonde curls, and she carries eggs and bacon on a plate in one hand and in the other a cup of milk. I can smell the milk and the bacon as she bends towards me. Nan is calling her back to the caravan. I don't want her to go. I want her to stay with me. Please, Mum, stay with me. But she goes back up the steps of the caravan. All the time my Nan is talking to her.

'Mum, you've forgotten my knife and fork.'

'Come and fetch it!' shouted Nan.

But Mum was already coming towards me laughing.

As she bends towards him she blots out his sun but absorbs all the heat and he lifts his arms in a dizzy fit of thrilling happiness.

As his fingers touch her hair he feels a heat rush into his feet and up through his body and so terrific is his sense of joy he is dizzy and leans his head back against the trunk of the tree.

He hears the sea rumble on the shingle and the shingle answer with a scattering of pebbles.

So dazzled by her hair as his fingers reach out and

touch it. His heart swells too quickly and heat rushes up his body. Dizzy, he leans his head back against the tree.

Now it is winter and the cold here is bitter. I ring when I can. She won't really talk when Jeff's there. I don't think I can bear it much longer.

CLEANING

On Mondays I go to my lovely lady. It's only a couple of hours so I leave Gladys in bed, she doesn't go to the Day Centre Mondays and Fridays.

I open the door with my own key and I say, 'Good morning, Mrs Holtby. How's your son?'

And then she asks me how mine is and how my mother is. She always asks after my mother every week and I like it. Then I take my coat off and my shoes and put on some slippers because she's got pale carpets. Her house is all white and pastel shades.

'Have you done anything exciting over the weekend?' I said.

'Yes, I went to a friend's hundredth birthday party in Sutton, and she's still got all her faculties only she's a bit stiff on her legs.'

She drove all the way and she's eighty-two years old

and her car is a ten-year-old Renault and it's immaculate. She drives all over.

Then she said, 'Oh Joy, thank goodness you put that card through my door. Thank goodness I've got you.'

'Thank you.'

'Now I've dropped all my letters on the floor, what a silly old cow I am. I call myself a silly old cow sometimes.'

'I call myself much worse than that,' I said, picking them up for her.

So upstairs I go and I do her bathroom first. I took her shower curtain down last week and washed it. That hadn't been done for years. She stays downstairs tiddling about and I clean the bath and basin and toilet, though they aren't really dirty. I like doing the spare room, it's wine red with a lime-green duvet cover. It looks rich. She's so spotless it makes your eyes turn out.

Then I come down into the kitchen. She sits writing a letter. Everything in the kitchen is white.

'Joy, I must tell you what I had for tea the other day. I made pancakes and maple syrup. They were delicious.'

I'm cleaning the cooker now and polishing it. It doesn't really need cleaning, it's shining anyway. She's got an emerald-green carpet in the passage, pure wool. It comes up beautifully when I hoover it. I take the rubbish out round the back and get a breath of fresh air and look at her garden – there's always something there even in the winter. She hangs all her underclothes out on the line when she washes them and they're snow white. I wish Gladys was like her. Then when I come back in she's made me a cup of coffee and we sit and talk. I like Mondays. I like going to Mrs Holtby's. Her house is so pretty. So that's Mondays.

On Tuesdays I do the Executive's house. When I get there I unlock the garage and turn the first alarm off. Then I go inside and turn the other alarm off and I mustn't do it wrong or the police will come and that will cost her seventy-five quid, she said. So I do the kitchen first. She's left me a list of what she wants me to do and in what order. Kitchen first, put all the chairs on the table. Wash the sides down. Wash the floor then seal it with polish. Wait for that to dry. Then downstairs toilet. Put the bleach in the toilet and leave it to take. Hoover the carpet and wipe all the sills down. Finish the kitchen then into the dining room. Polish the table (a great big fucking table . . . all heavy oak). Dust the computer. BUT BE SURE NOT TO UNPLUG IT. She's put this in great big letters on her note. Polish the sideboard. Then the hall. Hoover all the hall right through. Dust down the walls in case of cobwebs. Wipe all the glass in the pictures. Use a little spray to make them shine. Flick the feather duster all round. Then the lounge. Dust the glass shelves, hoover, polish the furniture, dust the picture frames, hoover the carpet. Hoover the stairs. She writes all this out for me but I don't always read it.

We've got to the first landing now. Two bathrooms to clean and three bedrooms. Make sure it's all polished. Spray first and then polish the great big mirror. Up the next flight of stairs again. Oh I forgot, empty all the bins.

Then at the top is the girls' playroom. Put the dolls away, hoover the carpet, wipe the window-sills (fucking sweet papers all over the place and I hate that, really gets on my nerves).

It's a big house and it takes me about three hours flat out to get through it and I'm worn out. I could have a cup of coffee but I'd rather keep going and get home. It's too big, this house.

At the end of the note she usually puts, 'When you have done all the necessaries if you have time clean the brass, or turn out the kitchen drawers or do the ironing.' I don't really like this job.

Wednesdays it's the Chinese lady. Another fucking three-storey house. First her kitchen, wash that thoroughly with bleach. Then I go upstairs and change all the beds and come down and put all the sheets in the washing machine.

At the very top of the house she has that futon bed. Then dust and polish and hoover all the way through. Come down and empty the hoover bag if it's full. Dust all the little shelves then down the passage and into the office. Another load of fucking hoovering and clean all the sides down.

She's got an open-plan lounge, clean that, lovely drape curtains in there. I enjoy that. I polish everything and dust all the plants. Then I take the washing out and hang it in the garden for her to bring in later. Then I finish the kitchen. Clean the microwave. Make sure the hob's clean. Empty the bin, wash the floor, clean and polish the fronts of the glass cupboards.

Then there's my Thursday lady, Mrs Brook. She's eighty-five, she dances around like a two year old, her furniture is all mahogany. Her silver is spotless and there isn't one bit of dust in her house.

When I get there she gives me a cup of tea. Her husband

has gone to play golf. Then she pulls everything out of the drawers and together we fold and tidy it away again and if she comes across anything she doesn't want she gives it to me. She's got a great big window and the sun shines straight through on to the blood-red carpet and the pink settee. She's got a mahogany coffee table with a glass top, fucking old-fashioned standard lamps, the shades go all crooked when I dust them. She sits and plays the piano while I polish and she sings, 'When Irish eyes are smiling . . . tra la . . .'

Sometimes she gets up and dances. She asked me if I liked dancing and I told her, 'Only when I'm drunk.' She has striped curtains, beige and maroon tied back with big sashes and snow-white nets. Upstairs there's the bathroom and two bedrooms with old-fashioned silk bedspreads.

Last week it was her sixtieth wedding anniversary and there was this great big jug of daffodils on the table and she and her husband were having breakfast.

'Come and have a cup of coffee with us, Joy,' she said.

I wished I had a house like that and that it was my wedding anniversary. I'd make it really beautiful too.

On Fridays I stay in bed. Jeff brings me a cup of tea before he goes to work and I drink it and go back to sleep or at least I pretend to be asleep in case Gladys comes in.

'Are you awake, Joy?'

'No, Mum, not yet,' I say. 'Go back in your own house.'

But this morning she came flying through the door. She was terrified. Her smoke alarm had gone off and frit the guts out of her. I go back with her into her house. The toast is burning and the alarm is shrieking. She can't handle it.

'Take that fucking thing down.'

I climbed up on her chair and took the battery out. Jeff fitted it up because I was worried she might set fire to herself when she falls asleep with a cigarette in her mouth.

When I was little I was very timid. Mum was very domineering. I was frightened of the dark and of being anywhere without her. What she said went. It has to be done how she said. It's always been like that. It's bred into you. I'll have to try and put the battery back in when she's not there.

'Give me your hand, Gladys.'

I got down.

'Do you remember Maisie?'

'Mum, I was only a tiny girl when you were friends with Maisie. How could I remember her?'

As a matter of fact I did remember Maisie. She had black hair and white sling-back shoes. I can remember her because I loved her shoes.

'Your shoes put me in mind of her.'

I wanted to scream. My shoes are nothing like that.

'No, Mum, her shoes were in your era not in my era. Times have changed. People have moved on. People are dead. You're an old woman now and you must sit back and let younger people take over.'

'Your trouble is you're spoilt and it's all your father's fault.'

'I'm going back to bed.'

I got into bed but I couldn't rest. I felt guilty. I could hear her coming in and out of my kitchen. I thought back to the time when Dad was alive and I was the apple of his eye. I thought about my lovely job and how I'd titivate myself before I went to work. I miss titivating myself. I'd hang out my clean clothes the night before.

I never wore the same thing two days running. First I'd have a wash and then I'd put the mirror on the kitchen table, drink my tea, smoke my fag, then I'd get down to titivating myself. First I'd put a bit of make-up on my face, only light, nothing heavy, then I'd do my eyes, inky-black mascara with a long brush, a tiny bit of eye shadow, different colour according to my mood. Mink brown was one of my favourites but I liked sea-shell pink and balmy blue. That made me think of holidays and there was a very soft green that glinted when I blinked. I liked that one, specially if I was wearing green shoes.

Then I'd plug in my machine and I'd get dressed and when it was good and hot I'd tong my hair, eat a bit of toast and last thing of all put on my lipstick, pearls on my ears, clip them on, one two, and my little pearl necklace around my neck. I'd leave the house at twenty-past eight regular every morning, get in my car, put my music on and drive away. Rod Stewart might be singing, 'Will I see you tonight?' or, 'Someone loves you, honey,' and I'd drive along through the park, wondering what the day would bring.

I miss my punters, talking to them when they're down. You get such clever people in there who can't get jobs. You don't get jobs on intelligence and exams alone, you have to have flair. Personality, that's what gets you on, and when you're down that all goes to pot.

I felt important there. I was somebody, and they were somebody to me. We bounced off each other. One day I went with a terrible hangover. Brian had to do all my stats and through-flow. I wasn't up to it. Every day was different.

I couldn't get back to sleep. I was angry. What had happened to my life?

THE NIGHT JOY LEFT BIG TOM TWENTY YEARS AGO

It had been hot all day. Clammy hot, sweaty hot. It was Joy's thirtieth birthday and she noticed some tiny lines around her eyes. She cleaned the flat in her bare feet. It was still hot when it got dark. Damp under her tits hot. Jonny was away on the school journey. He didn't want to go, poor little bugger, in case he wet the bed. Joy wouldn't have made him go. It was Big Tom insisted. They had had a row about it and he had hit her in the mouth. So Jonny went.

Tom came in angry. His brother was with him. It was late.

'I've got news for you. Good news!' he said.

'What's that, Tom?'

'Your old mate Dave is dead. Topped himself in Parkhurst yesterday. Old Rylands found him hanging by the neck from his window bar like a dead chicken in a butcher's window.'

* * *

The room started turning round very slowly. I opened my mouth to cry out but nothing came. I felt tears shoot out of my eyes. I'd really loved Dave. Tom stood sneering at me. His brother was beside him, watching.

So I turned my back. It was then he blew up. He slung a big heavy decanter at me. It missed and shattered on the floor and that's when he came towards me.

'I'm going to kill you,' he said, 'and then you can join him.'

I ran into the bedroom and locked the door. He punched a hole right through it. His brother hung on to him and I ran out past him, down the stairs, out into the middle of the night along Sheen Lane.

Tom ran after me but his brother knocked him down and sat on him and I got away. I had on a little pair of shorts and a bikini top. No shoes, my feet were bleeding where I'd stepped on broken glass and I ran and I ran.

There was a great big moon floating in the sky. It lit up the empty road. It was three o'clock in the morning. Joy was crying as she ran. The tarmac glistened and gleamed in the moonlight like a black river. She could smell her sweat mixing with the smell of warm tarmac. Some bright silver trees leant over the road.

A black man stopped in his white BMW.

'Hop in!' he said and he gave me a lift over to Gladys's and I rang her door bell. She was with old Arthur then. I couldn't speak. I was trembling. I was ill.

'Get in with us,' she said.

I got into bed. Arthur slept on one side of the bed. My

Mum slept in the middle and I slept the other side of her. I was shaking, I couldn't keep still. She cuddled me up.

'The bastard! Wait till I see him!'

As if she could do anything.

Next morning there was blood all over the sheets where my feet had bled. I hadn't even felt it. I went and collected my clothes when Tom was out, Gladys came with me, and I never went back. He tried to get me back many times but I never went back.

Jonny and I went to live with Mum and I got a divorce. We stayed with her till the council gave me a flat on the same estate. Later, when Jonny had left home, I did an exchange for a one-bedroom right next door to Gladys. She was still at work then. I think it was the baths . . . or was it the kiosk?

I had plenty of lovers but none of them stuck. I don't know if it were me or them. Perhaps I missed Dave and I do get bored quickly and then they get on my nerves.

Then years later, when I'd almost given up hope, I met Jeff.

Jeff got out of the cab of his dry-cleaning van. He was wearing cavalry-twill trousers and a lovely shirt.

'Coming in for a cup of tea?'

We drank the tea. I went and sat on his lap facing him, my legs either side of his.

'You know, Jeff, I fancy you.'

He began to sweat. I kissed him. Then I took my blouse off and showed him my tits. It was a boiling hot summer evening. The sun was just going down shining on the flats opposite and sending a bright glow through the windows.

I looked at him. The sweat poured off him. He was a big fellow. I like fat men. I think fat men can look after me. He touched my tits.

'I've got to go home,' he said.

We didn't have sex that first time. I didn't want sex. I wanted loving.

A few days after he asked me out.

I was wearing my short leopardskin coat. Jeff wore his blazer and I made him put a red handkerchief in the pocket. I had this wish that he'd win lots of money and we could go to a beautiful hotel and make love. Just get on a plane, and fuck off. That was when Jeff was fat. He's lost a lot of weight since then worrying over me.

THE CHIROPODIST

Glad and Joy sat in Gladys's flat drinking tea and eating ham rolls, waiting for the chiropodist.

'You've got to change that dress. You've got egg all down it.'

'I'll wear my black-and-white one.'

'That's dirty too. Take that off and put your blue one on. That's nice and warm.'

The telephone rang and it was Teddy.

'Come along when you like. She's waiting for the chiropodist.' Joy called, 'Ted's coming up later, Mum. He's got a pie for you.'

Gladys came hurrying in.

'I'd better put the potatoes on.'

She hadn't fastened her dress.

'Hold on let me zip you up,' said Joy.

Gladys took the tea things into the kitchen and washed up. Her bony white feet were bare in the beige slippers. She came back into the sitting room, looking around as if she'd forgotten something. A fag hung from her mouth, ash dropped on to the carpet. She wiped around the cut-glass ashtray and straightened the lace on the back of the settee. She talked to herself, 'Now that's done . . .'

She went out again and came back with a cup of tea, swilling the milky sugary mixture into the saucer.

'Sorry I've spilled it.'

Glad put the cup down and scratched her head.

'What have we got here? Have a look.'

She bent over so Joy could inspect her head. Carefully Joy pulled aside the thin hair.

'Nothing there, Mum, absolutely nothing, it's like a baby's scalp. Pure pink.'

Meanwhile, Janey the chiropodist was on her way. Past the Nissen hut library, past the row of shops half boarded up, she came. Outside the greengrocers stood a bucket of damp mauve chrysanthemums and a basket of yellow sprouts. It began to drizzle and Janey hurried up the concrete ramp and rang the bell.

'There she is,' said Joy.

Gladys sat in the armchair. Janey sat on a stool, a blue towel on her knees.

'I haven't had my feet done since I lived in Fulham.'

'That was twenty-six years ago, Mum. Dad's been dead twenty-five years. You came last month, didn't you, Janey?'

'That's right.'

Janey squirted between the toes with surgical spirit. A little blonde ponytail glistened on her back. Gladys sat bolt upright.

'I shall be like a fairy, won't I?'

Her nobbily foot rested Queen-like in the young woman's lap. Joy stood by and watched.

'They smell, Mum, because you don't wash them properly.'

'My feet don't smell.'

'The skin gets a bit waterlogged between the toes,' said Janey tactfully. 'That's why I spray the surgical spirit. Dries them out nicely.' She filed Gladys's toenails. 'Best not to cut them in case you catch the skin.' Gladys winced. 'Keep still, dear, I won't hurt you.'

Glad looked up at Joy beside her.

'She's doing a lovely job, Mum. Would you like a drop of orange, Janey?'

'Yes please. Once a week get a soft toothbrush and scrub between the toes. It gets rid of all the dead skin. Then spray it with surgical spirit.'

She took the silver scalpel and gently scraped the skin from between Gladys's toes. Joy fetched her a glass of cold orange.

'I can wear my high-heels now, can't I?' said Gladys.

'You should really wear lace-ups,' said Janey.

'I bought you a lovely pair of white lace-ups, Mum. What happened to them?'

'Those white ones? I threw them down the chute! I was tipping the rubbish and they went down,' said Glad.

'I bet they're in the back of your wardrobe.'

Joy disappeared and moments later reappeared carrying a pair of flat white lace-ups.

'I don't like flat shoes,' said Glad.

'Put them on.' Joy knelt at Gladys's feet and put on one

of the shoes while Janey put on the other. 'Now stand up and see how that feels.'

Gladys stood.

'Like a load of lead. I won't go out in them. I'd fall arse over head.'

'Well, you can wear them indoors.'

'It's because I've got dainty ankles. These are clodhoppers.' Gladys did a little skip and jump. 'These feet have seen some dancing.'

'I'll bet they have,' said Janey.

Ted came in and put his pie in the kitchen and sat in a chair in the corner.

'Nearly finished, Ted,' said Joy.

'Don't mind me.'

Ted didn't take up a lot of space. He'd lived all his life with his mother who died last year at ninety-five. Now he kept company with Gladys. Before she had had the fall they used to go to the pub. Now he brought her in a hot pie or fish and chips or a packet of fags.

On the wall hung a framed photograph of Joy on her twenty-first birthday. Her blonde hair is piled on top of her head Madame Pompadour-style and she wears an ocelot wrap draped over her shoulders.

'Lovely photo,' said Janey.

'That's me,' said Gladys, 'when I was young. My mother had thirteen children, I was the youngest. Jack and Rose, I don't know what they died of, I never asked. Rose had a stroke. Emmy died of cancer. She was very gay. The gayest girl you could ever have known. Ben died in Canada going on for ninety-one. He'd been out there since he was twenty-seven. Never came home no more, not even to die. Then come Sid, then come Jack. Sid died of old age in Fulham. Jack died . . . oh where was that bleeding place? I forget where he died. Then come Alice. She died in Hampton Court. She was a flower seller and a drinker. Me and her were good friends. Then come Rose. Rose lived in Fulham. She married Barney. She was never right after that. He was too cocky. She had a stroke and died. I came after Rose. The last to come and the last to go.'

Joy took the blue towel with all the bits of toe-nail wrapped inside it and shook it in the bin. Janey gathered up her instruments and packed them in her black bag.

Joy saw her to the door.

'That photo you liked.'

'Yes?'

'It's me.'

'I guessed it was.'

'Ben, Aggie, Ethel, Sid, Ginny . . . she died in an old people's home . . . she was ninety-four. Sid, I don't know what became of Sid. He died, I expect. Emmy, she died. Ginny . . . Rose, she died. Jack, he died of pneumonia. Alice died young. She went to America and died. She sent me a fox fur from New York,' said Gladys.

Ted scratched his moth-eaten chin, and stared hard at his newspaper folded back to the racing page while Gladys fetched plates and then couldn't remember where she'd put the ketchup. Ted found it for her in the fridge.

'I'm going next door, Mum. I'll be back in a little while to give you your bath.'

Joy left them to it.

When she got indoors she put the kettle on and laid a tray with her pretty tea set. Then she made a pot of tea and took it into her front room and set it down on the table. She poured herself a cup and sat down on her beautiful sofa and got out her favourite letters. Then she read them, one after the other, as hungrily as she had the first time.

Dear Joy,

This is a short line to let you know that I have been successful in my interview with British Rail and have landed a job in the Travel Centre at Richmond Station. I start next week.

Naturally I am both delighted and relieved at finding work again after eighteen months of twiddling my thumbs, and I cannot let the occasion pass without expressing my sincere and heartfelt thanks to Job Club and to you in particular, Joy. You obviously provided the spark that set the wheels of my train into motion, if you will excuse the pun.

The atmosphere at your Job Club is so relaxed that you are able to think clearly about your potential value to employers, and to share your shortcomings and misfortunes with others in the same boat as yourself. I think it is the feeling that nobody is getting at you that puts you in the right frame of mind to go about the serious and immensely difficult business of finding a job. I know that without attending the Job Club and having the luck to fall on you as the leader I would never have been provided with the impetus and drive that enabled me to go to my interview with the degree of self-confidence which is so necessary in seeking employment these days. You were a figure of authority and a friend.

Carry on with the excellent work, Joy, as soon as your mother is out of danger. You have obviously found your true vocation in life. I will think of you every time I hear the salute Hip Hip Hurray!

Yours very truly, Brian.

Joy folded it and put it carefully away in its envelope. Then she took out the next one.

Dear Joy,

First let me send you my best wishes for your mother's health and the hope that she has got over her fall. I am writing to say how very much I appreciated your guidance in securing further training in office procedures after such a long period in the 'wilderness'.

It almost goes without saying that your inimitable leadership of the Club was a source of inspiration to us all. You are a walking, talking dynamo and never failed to find time for an encouraging word with your honeyed tongue! You should be promoted as a 'role model' for all the clubs in the rest of the country.

Kindest regards always, Colin.

This too she folded very carefully and put away before she read the last letter.

Dear Joy,

Just to say thanks for everything. You're a one in a million, Joy, and I shall be eternally grateful for just knowing you. People never understand that able people can get as lacking in confidence as anyone else if their abilities are not being used and appreciated. And we all need love to keep us going, especially when we're down. It helped me enormously when you got me typing other people's c.v.s and making phone calls for them.

And you understood me in human terms, just as I was, not as a list of 'qualifications' and 'failures'. I stopped seeing myself as a list of negatives that had to be inevitable turn-downs by prospective employers.

I would never have got that c.v. written in a million years except for what I picked up from the Job Club and you.

I haven't got my ideal job, as you know. I still want to be working with people on that personal level. But I will be doing something that requires some of the other know-how qualities I have and it is useful and straight. It'll be good to be in the 'pool' again and to have something to live on into the bargain. Am I glad I wasn't daft enough not to join the Job Club. Thank you for being you!

Lots of love and a big hug, Lindy.

When she had finished reading Joy was overcome with a sinking feeling, a vast terror that she may never ever get back to work. Her manager had told her they couldn't, they wouldn't keep the job open and Peter, she knew, had taken her place. She lay back on the sofa.

I should have hung on to my job, popped in on her of an evening, done her washing and gone indoors and lain down in peace.

But she knew, in her heart, Glad would never have managed with her out at work all day and if she went into a home she wouldn't be looked after like Joy looked after her.

It's too late now. If I leave her she'll fucking die.

Joy rolled on to her stomach and wept. Then she slept.

When she woke it was already dim outside. She washed her face and went to bath Gladys. Ted had gone home.

Gladys wouldn't have a bath on her own now so Joy bathed her.

'Leave my clothes there.'

'No, Mum, I'm going to wash them.'

'They're not dirty.'

'You've had them on for seven days and seven nights.'

'Leave those stockings there, I can wear them tomorrow.'

'No, you've had them on for a week too, you've got to have clean ones.'

'They're not really dirty. I won't be two minutes in this bath. I'm not dirty.'

'Did you enjoy your afternoon with Ted?'

'He doesn't have nothing to say. I'm fucking glad when he's gone. He don't talk to you. He's no fun. I'm sure he's got another woman.'

Joy shook out the towels listening with half an ear.

'He won't get nothing off of me,' said Gladys.

Joy put the rack across the bath and Gladys heaved herself up on to it.

'Hang on tight.'

'Got me?'

'Yes, I've got you, Big Bertha. You know, you're not wasting away, Mum. That's one thing I can say for you. Mind you don't slip and dry properly so you don't catch cold.'

Gladys filled the basin with fresh cold water and washed her face. Joy handed her a towel.

'I enjoyed that,' said Glad.

'Sit still while I dry your back.'

She powdered under her boobs with Johnson's baby powder. She lifted them up . . .

'Cor, they're a ton weight.'

Gladys smiled.

'Here, remember when we went topless and caused all that attraction? I want my toe-nails red and my fingernails red, Joy.'

'I'll do them tomorrow.'

Joy got a clean petticoat to put over Glad's head.

'That's the one that clings. I don't like that one.'

She fetched another one.

'I like this one, is it a new one?'

'It's the one we got on Saturday at the boot sale in Putney.'

'Is it real silk?'

'I should think so for thirty p.'

'It feels like real silk. I don't want no stuff on my feet, she's done all that.'

'Put on your new dressing gown and try not to burn it with your cigarette.'

'I like this. Look at the cuffs. I'd like that Bert back.'

'He sent you a Christmas card.'

'Yes, he sent me a Christmas card. Nothing in it though, not even a fiver.' She stared in the mirror. 'I think I look old in this.'

'You are old. I'm going in to get the dinner ready. Jeff'll be home by now. You stay here and wash your knickers and your petticoat, that'll clean your nails. I'll call you when it's ready.'

'How old do you think I look, Joy?'

'You look old, Mum.'

'Do I look as old as Teddy?'

'Teddy's seventeen years younger than you!'

'But he looks older, doesn't he?'

'You look very well for your age but you are eighty.'

'I don't think I look eighty, do you?'

'You're lucky you ain't got much wrong with you.'

'When I die you've got to get rid of all my stuff.'

'Who'd fucking want it, Mum?'

'My dad never wanted me. He used to call me "Eyesore". "Come here, Eyesore," he'd say. Aggie was his favourite. He made a slave of my Rose. But me, he never liked me. He made me clean his boots. I had to get every bit of mud and cement out of the treads. He never took me out and about.'

'That was a long time ago, Mum.'

'I haven't got no future to talk about, have I?'

Joy rinsed out the bath.

'Put your slippers on and come along in a minute.'

'Do I look all right?'

'Yes, you look lovely.'

'You haven't even turned your head. By the way, I want to be buried, not cremated.'

'But if you're buried, Mum, who will come up and see you when I die?'

'What will become of you when I go, Joy?'

'I might go before you.'

'Well, if you die I die with you.'

'I know you would. There'd be no one to look after you. It frightens the life out of me.'

Gladys took a cigarette.

'I might have killed myself on those steps.'

'Well, you didn't. That's the last one, Mum. You can't have that one.'

But Gladys didn't hear so she lit up. And Joy hoped Jeff had got some indoors.

'Is the dinner ready yet, Joy?'

'Mum, you've had a hot pie.'

'Well, I'm hungry.'

She followed Joy along the walkway and into her flat. Jeff sat at the kitchen table studying the racing.

'Any good bets, Jeff?' said Gladys.

But Jeff didn't look up.

'I don't know if Maud's dead.'

Jeff went on studying the form.

'You spoke to her on the phone the other day, Mum. She rang you up.'

'Oh I forgot. I don't get out and about and I don't hear what's going on so I have to live with the memory of what has gone on, which is wrong. To me, that's wrong. If I live another six years I shall be happy.'

'But you've got to think what you'll be like in six years' time.'

'Well, none of us know.'

'Yes, but you've had a blow to the brain and you're confused.'

'Yes, but I'll come out of it again. I'll come out of it. You'll get confused when you get old. Everybody does.'

'Your deaf-aid is coming tomorrow, Mum. You can wear it indoors.'

'I don't want to wear it indoors because I can hear.'

'You can't hear.'

'I won't wear it. I'll tell you that.'

'It's very difficult for me having to shout.'

'No good getting it because I won't wear it.'

'Everybody has to shout at you. You don't know we're shouting because you're deaf.'

'I can hear you talking.'

'Yeah, because I'm shouting all the time.'

'You're not shouting. Is she shouting, Jeff?'

Jeff raised his head from his paper.

'She's talking loud, Glad.'

'Yes, loud but not shouting.'

'Sometimes it wears you out talking loud. It's only a tiny button. You must try it, Mum, for your own sake.'

'All right, I'll try it and if I don't like it I'll soon take it out. I'm my own guvnor. I don't like people telling me what to do. No, I've done what other people want me to do. Now I want to do what I want to do.'

I sorted the washing.

Tonight I just don't want to be with Gladys. Then I

resent Jeff because she gets on his nerves so I have to keep him happy and then I have to keep her happy and then I have to do the dinner and then I do the washing and then Jeff doesn't want his washing put in the machine with Mum's.

'Wash mine separate, Joy.'

I don't take no notice, in it all goes.

'Is the dinner ready yet, Joy?'

If I go like that I want to be put away.

THE SEX SCENE

Jeff and Joy sat at the kitchen table. They had spent all yesterday papering the bedroom with Gladys walking in and out. Now Jeff was teaching Joy how to do accounts. He hoped she might help him in the dry-cleaning business when he branched out on his own.

'I had to wear glasses from a very early age, Jeff. I wouldn't wear them because they wasn't pretty ones, they were National Health ones, and I said, "No, I'm not wearing them," and I didn't wear them so I couldn't see what was going on at school. I couldn't see the blackboard.'

Gladys looked through the window and seeing them sitting there she came in and stood by the table humming.

'When I was about thirteen or fourteen she bought me a pretty pair but it was too late then.'

'So, Glad, you didn't make her wear her glasses?' said Jeff.

'I told her to wear them.'

'She told me to wear them but I wouldn't and that was it. She didn't make me. Kids laugh at people wearing glasses.'

'I had a hell of a trouble with her when she was going to school over those glasses, Jeff. First she had the tin ones. I couldn't afford nothing else. She wouldn't wear them and that was it. She didn't like these ones and she didn't like those ones. I bought her some rim ones in the end. She wore them for a little while but she soon left them off.'

'I never liked wearing glasses.'

'Everybody used to think she was an angel. "Your Joy's a dear little soul," they'd all say. I didn't tell them about the glasses.'

Jeff laughed.

'I'm off,' he said. 'I'll see you later.'

'That paper's nice. Will you do mine when you've finished in there, Jeff?'

Jeff doesn't want it all the time so he didn't answer. He went pretending he didn't hear.

'He's getting deaf, Joy.'

'Come on, it's time to go across to the surgery.'

Gladys was pleased Jeff had gone. Pleased to have Joy to herself. And Joy, feeling Gladys's frail warmth through her thin coat as she linked her arm across to the surgery, wished she could be somewhere else.

They sat in the surgery waiting room. The walls were covered with posters about illness. DID YOU KNOW THAT HEPATITIS-A KILLED MORE PEOPLE WORLDWIDE THAN AIDS? PNEUMOCOCCAL PNEUMONIA? ARE YOU AT RISK? Joy felt a grey sludge descending on her, relentlessly filling her eyes, her ears, her nostrils. She could even taste it on her tongue. She'd had another telephone call from Jonny last night threatening to desert. What could she do about it? He was a man now and had to make his own way. He'd joined the Army. She hadn't wanted him to join up. He'd signed the deal. He had to stick to it. She couldn't have him home in a one-bedroom flat. She hadn't told Jeff because it hurt her when he criticised Jonny, it hurt very very much. No one knew how much.

Last night I lay awake and I imagined exactly what had happened to him. I even saw his funeral. Sometimes I'm so frightened I feel sick and I smoke so much I just want to lie down and sleep for a year.

Once in the nurse's room Gladys took off her shoes and stood, good as gold, on the weighing machine. She held her small stout body bolt upright, enjoying the attention. The nurse was young and wore a long skirt and for a moment Joy was shot through with a painful shaft of red-hot jealousy for her youth, for her prettiness, for her light-heartedness.

Gladys answered her questions cheerfully although she couldn't always hear what she was saying and Joy often interrupted which Glad didn't like. She knew more about her own body than Joy did and she liked the pretty nurse. Anyway, Joy was in a dodgy mood today. Glad smiled at her as she took her blood-pressure and the nurse smiled back.

'Very good, you can put your cardigan on again.'

'Thank you very much.'

Joy helped her on with her cardigan and they went home and put the kettle on.

'Here, your eyebrows are coming up ever so thick.'

'Do them then, Joy.'

Joy got Jeff's razor and peered closely at Gladys's face.

'Jeff will be wild if he knows you've used his razor,' said Glad.

'Well, don't tell him then, Mum.'

'Not if I remember, I won't. Don't use the tweezers. They hurt me.'

'I won't.' Joy shaped Glad's eyebrows with the razor. 'I'll make them all thin and elegant. You've got some long hairs. I won't shave those. I'll nick 'em off.'

'Fuck you!'

'I didn't hurt you.'

'Yes you did.'

'You can't have nothing on your face.' Gladys put her tongue inside her top lip and bulged it out so Joy could nick the hairs off her moustache. 'What about your nails?'

'Paint them red.'

'You're not having them red. I can't see when they're clean.'

'I want them red.'

So in the finish Joy did them red.

They drank their tea, then Joy went out on to the balcony to bring in the washing. Seagulls, straying from the Thames, settled on the giant dustbins and shouted their strangled sea-faring cry. The sky had opened up and the sun was sinking fast but as it sank it was dazzling bright, shining through broken clouds, and then, already quite high on the other side of the sky, she saw a full moon, a pale white blond moon. And the gleaming sun, streaking the edges of the black clouds pink on its descent, shone a brilliant farewell, lighting up the trees one last time, then the tower blocks as it passed, making everything desirable, everything beautiful. The white moon lay in wait. Joy watched, enchanted, and as she looked she felt her mood change, she breathed deeply and was soothed.

When I was thirteen I saved up thirteen shillings and I bought these green high-heeled shoes decorated with silver moons. I hid them and sneaked out in them one evening but Gladys saw me from the window and she shouted, 'You're not wearing them.' And I shouted back, 'You're jealous.' And she didn't speak to me for three days. And that night too, the moon had been up before the sun went down and later the sky had been festive with stars.

Soon after that it was my birthday and Gladys had all these lovely colours to go on her eyes what she got when she cleaned for a lady who worked at Gala's and I said, 'Let me have some of that green, Mum.' I knew it would set off my shoes. 'No,' she said. She was a cow to me sometimes.

Joy went indoors leaving the window wide to blow in the cold evening air.

'I'm going to have a bath now so go back to your house.'

'I think I've got fleas. I felt something in my eyebrow. I'm sure I've got one in my eyebrow. It's biting me like hell. Have a look and see what you can see.' Joy had a look. 'Put your glasses on. I think I've got one round the back of my neck. There's something there. I can feel it itching.'

'There's nothing there, Mum.'

'Have a look on the top of my head.'

'That's your brain. It's where you've had your fall, it's affected your thinking. Your hair's lovely. I did it with the flea comb yesterday.'

'What makes it itch then?'

'It's your nerves. And if you keep pulling at it you'll have no hair left. I'll see you later.'

Joy turned on the bath. She heard an aeroplane, through the open window, croon overhead. She took her clothes off. It was cold. She got in and wriggled right down into the hot scented water and lay still.

As she dried herself a chilly breeze tickled her naked skin. It excited her. She shut the window. She thought of Jeff and her thoughts grew and grew.

I slicked back my hair, really greased it dead flat. Then I put on my pink sunglasses, a black pearl choker, black all-in-one brassière and suspenders, black high-heeled shoes and long black satin gloves to above the elbow. I got them in Oxfam.

I rang Jeff on his mobile and I said, 'Get over here! Sharpish!' Then Mum came in and I quickly put on my old dressing gown.

'You just washed your hair?'

And I thought: Please don't keep talking to me, Gladys, I'll lose this sensation I've got.

'When Jeff comes you go because I want to be on my

own for a bit and he gets the 'ump if you're in here all the time.'

'Why?'

'Because we've been decorating all weekend and it's nice sometimes just me and him.'

'Are you going out?'

'No.'

'What have you done to your hair?'

'I've got conditioner on it.'

We go out on to the balcony where I can watch for Jeff's red van.

'You'll catch cold out here. There's Jeff's van ain't it?'

'Yes, that's Jeff's van so off you go.'

Glad stood there. Jeff came up the stairs. He came out on to the balcony.

'Hello, Jeff,' said Gladys.

'Hello, Glad.'

He's looking at me. He can see I've got my black stockings on under the dressing gown and then he knows.

'Had a bet today, Jeff?'

He's looking at me, so he doesn't answer her.

'I wish I were in Brighton,' she said.

I'm looking at him. I give him a look and poke my tongue out. It's freezing out on the balcony – I shiver.

At last she says, 'Well, I'll go now.'

She goes along into her own house and we go inside. He wanted to kiss me but I hadn't time for that.

'Pull the blinds down in the kitchen and bolt the door. Close your eyes and when I tell you you can open them.'

I took the dressing gown off and I sat on the kitchen table leaning back on my arms.

'Open your eyes.'

Well, the sweat started to pour off him even before he touched me.

'Now walk behind me.'

I walked slowly down the passage, swinging my hips, into the bedroom and I got up on the bed. I still wouldn't let him kiss me.

'I've waited weeks for this. Now I can't wait any longer. I need lots of men to satisfy me so put my mask on so I can't see you.'

He got it out of the drawer, the one we bought in Amsterdam. His hands were shaking. He could hardly fasten it.

We must have been in there two or three hours. I had dropped off. Someone is banging the door. I put my track suit on and go and open up. Glad stood there scratching her head.

'Whatever have you been doing? I've stood here banging. I couldn't open the door. These fleas aren't half biting me.'

JEFF SPEAKS

One freezing afternoon Jeff decided to take Joy to a flotation tank on Clapham Common that he'd heard about from a mate in the dry-cleaning business.

'This Saturday instead of going round the boot sales you're coming with me.'

'I won't drown, will I?'

'No, it's only six inches deep.'

Joy takes off her clothes and folds them neatly and puts them on the seat of the chair. Jeff hangs his over the back. It isn't a posh place. In fact they were told they should have brought their own towels. The young man with the ponytail finds them a couple of small ones with frayed ends.

'Don't let go of my hand.'

'I won't. Just shut your eyes and relax.'

Floating side by side in the dark warm water. Holding

her little bird-like hand as if I was holding just the thin bones, no flesh.

'My back is going to break in two,' said Joy. 'Don't turn out the light. I can't breathe.'

'Let go, let go, darling.'

'Ahh, I'm floating.'

The tips of her breasts, her nipples, protruded from the dark water.

Her knees, the bones of her hips, all bones like the small bunch of bones in my hand. I move my fingers between her fingers.

She sighs.

'Turn out the light, Jeff.'

I reach up and turn out the small dim light. Now we are in pitch black floating, the salty water the same temperature as the air, as our blood.

'Am I still here?'

'Yes, feel my hand.'

'I thought I might be dead.'

'You're alive.'

'Yes, I'm alive. I can hear my heart beating.'

'Lie quiet.'

Ahh. I'm so still.'

I hold the small hand while I listen to her breathing change and she sleeps. I don't want to sleep but to guard her sleep, her fragile hand in mine, and listen to her breathing. My princess sleeps and I lie beside her in the dark water very wide awake in the pitch silence.

Later we walk home holding hands. There is ice on the puddles. We stop under some trees near the flats and I look at her. Her face is washed clear, even her eyes are a lighter blue. Salt water has washed her eyes, pale-blue stones washed up on the beach . . . bleached into stillness.

GLADYS SPEAKS

Gladys came into my house.

'Can you make me a cup of tea?'

'No, Mum, make one in your own house. Jeff'll be home in a minute.'

'I'm not in his way.'

'Where's Teddy then?'

'He's not been near or by. I bet he's had a win and he doesn't want to give me nothing. I'm not giving him nothing neither, he's got another bird.'

And sure enough a few days earlier, I had seen Ted talking to a ginger woman down by the shops and they went off together. 'Don't tell your mother you seen me,' he says to me the next day. I didn't say nothing to Gladys, I didn't want to upset her but she's got her suspicions.

Gladys kissed me.

'Good-night love, I won't be back no more. You think I'm a bloody nuisance to keep running in and out so I won't do it.' I didn't answer.

'I don't come in much really, do I?'

'You come in a lot. Last Sunday Jeff counted and you were in and out thirty-eight times.'

'Yes, I come in a lot, I know, but I'm not what you call hung round you all the time, am I?'

'Not really. Don't come in no more tonight, Mum, I'll see you in the morning.'

As a matter of fact Jeff was on late shift tonight but somebody, long ago, put guilt on me and I've let it overgrow and tonight I wasn't going to listen, so I'll tell you what I did. I put on my silk pyjamas then I made myself two bits of toast. I put cheese on it. I got an onion and spread it all over, then two bits of tomato very thinly sliced. I made myself a cup of tea, took my fags, and there I was, sitting up in bed watching *Casablanca* and eating my toast. When I had finished I put the tray on the floor, snuggled down inside the duvet and went to sleep.

I was at peace. I knew Gladys was all right and Jeff would wake me up when he came in later.

Gladys went back to her own house and lit a fag. She looked out of her window at the tower blocks, spaced at intervals down the hill, each separate, high and grey and clear in the evening gleam of street lights.

She needed to do some thinking.

Sometimes I try not to go in her house but I can't help it, I've got to go, something tells me I've got to go.

She took a pull on her fag and opened the window on to the balcony and went out.

The starlings were flocking together in the skies and a crowd dropped to rest in the lime tree where they twittered like schoolchildren waiting for the coach to take them on an outing. As she watched, the light glittered on the windows opposite then dusk fell. Dark clouds gathered and ran across the sky.

She went inside and sat down. She stood up.

I walk in the front room and back again. When I see her I'm all right. Once she's in I know I'm all right but when she goes out and she's out a long time I start to think: I wonder if anything's happened . . . I know she's a good driver but all the good drivers in the world make mistakes. But she's in tonight.

Gladys imagined Joy pottering about in her kitchen, polishing her copper chest, making everything shine. She would see her tomorrow. Tomorrow was quite soon when you thought about it. Then it rushed into her head how Joy had mentioned yesterday, all casual, she fancied moving away.

If she does that my life will be finished. If she moved away I don't know what I'd do. My mother's mother was a gypsy. Terrible wanderer, perhaps Joy takes after her. Her name was Smart, circus people, Romany gypsies from Battersea. I could have trained to be an acrobat because I was wiry and I could jump but my mother wouldn't part with me.

She remembered learning to tap dance in Hammersmith.

I got in with this woman called Madame Victor – she took to me and put me in a show. My dad heard about it and he gave me a hiding. I would have been out on the roads now. I would have been an acrobat in the circus but he stopped it. 'You're not going to make a whore of my daughter,' he said.

And Gladys saw herself joining the circus. She saw herself dressed in silver with silver shoes high up above the crowd . . . a star.

I cried my eyes out. I was thirteen and I ran away from home. I stayed away for three or four days. I was never the same after. It was my ambition. Instead I stuck with my mum. Three times a week we'd go to the pictures together. We had three different picture palaces, Fulham Broadway, Hammersmith Broadway, Putney Bridge. We were never without one another. Mind you, it was cheaper then. It was only sixpence.

My mother came to live with me when she was old. We was like two doves in a pot. I can see her now standing on the doorstep in her overall waiting for me to come back from work. Whatever happened, Joy must never move away.

Gladys felt a sharp stabbing pain in her leg and she sat down.

I can't walk like I used to.

And again she thought about her mother.

She had a boyfriend named George with a moustache. She'd take her jug over the road for her Guinness. When she couldn't do that no more she took to her bed. She was seventy-eight when she took to her bed. She wouldn't get up. She used to have her two pints of Guinness every day. I used to fetch it for her. Two years she stayed in bed. Then she got up and fell in the fire.

She fell in the fire and burnt herself and that was the end. I had her put in a home.

It was a long way to Norwood. Me and my Gin took her. We cried all the way. Soon after she was dead.

Brief moments of light flared from a bonfire behind a wall not far off. Gladys thought again of Joy only a few yards away putting on her pyjamas – she knew she liked putting on her silk pyjamas in the evening. She could smell the smoke and hear the voices of children. Below her balcony some passers-by were talking. She heard a young woman's laughter ring like a bell, clear and happy. She imagined some fellow taking her arm.

Perhaps they're on their way home from the pub, lucky sods.

I've got that pain again. It must be indigestion. I eat things that I'm not supposed to eat. I'm a naughty girl really.

You don't want to go where you're not wanted and get told off, do you? If she told me not to come in I wouldn't go. I mean I don't do no harm to her. I only go in to see if she's all right, yes, I do call in for five minutes, it's a break to get out of my own house. It's a break, that's all it is, a little break and it does me the world of good just to have that little tiny break. I mean I go in there and have a little tiny conversation and I'm relieved again and I can get on with what I'm doing.

She burped.

That's better. It was only wind.

She looked at the clock, it was ten now. She thought she may as well pop in and say good-night. She unlocked Joy's front door. The lights were out in the kitchen and the front room but she could see a light under the bedroom door. She knocked hard.

'You awake? I've just come to say good-night.'

'Leave it!' said Jeff.

They were making love. But Joy couldn't, she had to go to Glad, and by the time she came back they'd lost it, and it was the first time in ages.

'Bloody hell!' said Jeff.

He got dressed and went and sat in the front room. Joy put on her dressing gown and followed him.

'Come back to bed, Jeff.'

'I couldn't if I wanted to,' he said. 'I'm too bloody angry.'

Joy went back to bed on her own and tried to sleep. Much later Jeff crept in and wrapped his feet around hers.

Gladys took off her dressing gown. She could go to bed now she'd seen Joy. A breeze got up and died again. High in the sky the swagging clouds broke for a moment. She glimpsed a star, big and bright, and then it was hidden.

Gladys got into bed and settled down.

She doesn't really want me in when Jeff's there.

One of her curlers is jabbing into her head. She'll have to tell Joy in the morning to try and buy her some softer ones.

Later she woke and heard a roaring and a rumbling. The thunder was shaking right through the flat. The wardrobe rattled and Gladys was afraid it might fall. She got out of bed. Outside the window lightning slashed the sky so bright her new dress hanging on the balcony to air lit up vermilion red. The wind was thudding and booming. She went to the door and opened it and peered out. The rain was coming down in a single sheet. She scuttled the few yards along the covered walkway to see if Joy's kitchen light was burning.

She must have been woken by the thunder.

As she hurried out the wind unleashed a fearsome gust that slammed the door behind her. She heard it go.

Out of the dark sky the rain hurtled under the walkway in a stinging deluge drenching her pink nightdress. She gasped for breath and rattled on Joy's door but perhaps Joy, hating thunder which once again rumbled threateningly above then a crash and more lightning splitting the sky, had put her head firmly under the pillow and intended to keep it there till the storm passed, till morning even. Glad pressed her wet face against Joy's kitchen window, cupping it in her shaking hands, and prayed to God she'd see Joy in her dressing gown putting on the kettle, and Joy would see her. The kitchen was dark. She saw nothing till another flash of lightning lit up the window and she let out a howl of despair as the wind blew a bank of rain against her back and wildly she rattled on the letter-box.

'Help me, Joy!'

Joy in her dreams heard that last cry and woke and struggled up and out from under the duvet and uncurled her feet from round Jeff's legs and stumbled half asleep into the kitchen and heard her mother's wailing mix with the sound of plummeting rain. She opened the door and, thrust forward by the wind, Gladys flew in and stood gasping and dripping on the kitchen floor. Her sparse white hair clung to her pink face and her pink nightdress clung transparently around her stout body wet wet wet.

'Oh Mum, wherever have you been?'

Jeff shouted from the bedroom, 'What the fuck does she want now?'

Next morning there was a rainbow.

Christmas came but there wasn't much gilt on the gingerbread. They were all short of money and Joy hated the scrimping and saving and queuing for the cheapest oranges in the market, and when she got them home they weren't the juicy ones she had wanted. Jonny got three days leave but he wasn't his old carefree self. He'd changed.

That Christmas was a miserable Christmas. Ted lost his teeth down the toilet. It was a new set too and this was the first time he'd had them in. He sat in his chair all forlorn. Then Joy burnt her hand getting the turkey out with the oven mitts Gladys had made up at the Day Centre, 'All hand-stitched, Joy, by me.'

Then Gladys got a black eye when Jonny was demonstrating what he could do with the juggling set Joy had given him.

'Look, Nan!'

She had looked and one of the balls had come down clonk on her eye.

Then Jonny had an argument with Jeff, in spite of Joy desperately trying to keep everyone happy, and shut himself in the front room so nobody could watch the telly and then Jeff, fed up with the lot of them, ran out and joined his mates in the pub.

'Least said, soonest mended,' he quoted when he returned several hours later.

And that was Christmas.

THE FLEAS

Joy was scrubbing her kitchen floor. She knelt, a bucket of soapy water beside her, and scrubbed the white tiles to make them gleam. She'd woken from a dream with this desire for gleaming white, shining white.

Gladys came in scratching her head.

'Stop, Mum, the floor's wet.'

Joy lifted high the scrubbing brush to bar her entry. And Gladys, seeing the upraised scrubbing brush and with both hands in her itchy hair, stopped. She stood quite still, staring at the scrubbing brush and Joy went back to scrubbing.

'Joy, Joy, I know what I want to tell you. It was my dad.' Gladys sat down. 'My mum was ill. She had to be taken away to hospital. I had a letter come from school that I had to go up the cleansing station. I was about ten years old. He said, "What's this? You got fleas? Come here and let me look in your head." Then he finds a flea. He shouted, "You're not bloody bringing your fleas in here!" He's got hold of the floor brush and put some Harris's Pomade on it and he's scrubbed my head till it bled and I was screaming aloud and my mum was laying ill in hospital and my head was covered in blood where the bristles had torn it and he boxed my ears and oh did I cry.

'I ran out into the road and I was crying all the way up the hospital and I showed my mum where my scalp was all torn. She said, "I'm coming home," and she discharged herself. "What have you done to my baby, you bastard?" and she hit him on the head and he gave her a black eye and ran out of the house.'

Gladys sat on a chair. Tears poured out of her eyes.

'I don't know where these tears are coming from, Joy, but I can't seem to put a stop to them.'

And she cried some more.

Joy got up off her knees to fetch the tissues.

'Don't cry, the old bastard's dead and you haven't got any fleas now, I promise you. Your hair looks beautiful, it's all grown. Those pills are doing wonders.'

'I wouldn't be without you, Joy.'

'I wouldn't be without you either, Mum.'

'I won't be going in a home will I, Joy?'

'No, you won't be going in a home.'

'I'm no trouble to you,' said Gladys.

'No, you're no trouble to me, Mum.'

'You'd have been petrified of him. He was a bastard and I was an eyesore to him. He didn't want me. He didn't want me from a baby. He hated me.'

And Gladys cried all over again.

'I'll make a cup of tea and we'll have five minutes,' said Joy.

Gladys sat on Joy's sofa, she leant back against the cushions and thought about her mother. So she told Joy who came back with two cups of tea.

'If I went out with a fellow I'd bring my mum home a drop of beer in a bottle. She'd be laying on my bed waiting for me to come in: "Is that you? What you got?" Sometimes I'd bring her home some fish and 'tatoes and we'd eat it together, her in her nightgown. My dad would be in bed asleep, or if he was awake, she'd pretend to be telling me off: "Who do you think you are coming in at this time of night?" We'd sit together in the dark.'

So sat Joy and Gladys drinking their tea while outside the sky was dim with chill and drizzle. Gladys dozed off and Joy went back to her floor.

When Gladys woke she followed Joy back to the kitchen.

'I used to wash my mum's doorstep so I could watch who was going past. That's how I come to meet Wally Cobler. He's dead now. I had some games with him. Nobody knows.'

Gladys sat down and lit a fag. She was happy now looking on.

'I had a gang then, Joy. There was Dolly Sivers, me, Shussy Parsons, Morty Leyland, Daisy Webb, Phyllis Adrian, who else, Queenie Miles. There was about eight of us. They might all be dead for all I know. I wouldn't know 'em now.

'We'd go up the cinema on a Saturday afternoon. We'd

take a whole row of seats. The girl that used to come round with the sweets took to me, she used to give me the sweets, not the others. There'd be Willy Webb, Percy Waldrop, Freddie Green, Harry Arbour, all them were my schoolmates. I don't know where they are now but I expect they're all dead and if they ain't they can't remember. I'd love to meet them all but I don't suppose I ever will, not if they're all dead.'

And Joy down on her knees polished her white tiles till they shone.

The telephone rang and it was Jonny. He'd got into a fight and he was scared he'd get locked up and miss his next leave. Joy reassured him as best she could but she felt sick at heart.

'I'm frightened he might run away, Mum. I can't have him moving in with me with only one bedroom and Jeff here. But then again I can't turn him away. I can't see him in the street. I could never see him out.'

'He's a naughty boy,' said Gladys. 'Wait till I get hold of him.'

All those guns, supposing something went wrong? Supposing someone got shot? Supposing Jonny were to die?

And Joy went rigid with fright, it seemed as if her heart stopped beating, so stiff she was with fear.

But she only said, 'He's a grown man, Mum.' And Joy put on her coat. Suddenly she had to get out. 'I'm going over to Carol's.'

'I'll come with you.'

'No, I'm going on my own. I'll see you later.'

Then she flew over in the Fiat to her friend Carol's,

on the far side of the estate, and said, 'Carol, I've got to get out,' and they went shopping.

She fancied making some little flouncy curtains for her kitchen. She bought some pale-lemon glazed cotton and a lime-green ribbon to make a border. She couldn't afford it but she didn't care. And Carol bought a new duvet cover. She couldn't afford it either. Then they went back to Carol's flat to use her sewing machine.

Carol was glum. She told of her daughter Tracy who had bought her one-bedroom flat from the council. She and Bob had both been working when they got married, but now they had two kids and couldn't afford a bigger flat and the council wouldn't rehouse them and they had huge service charges and Tracy was seeing the doctor about depression. Joy told of Jonny and how he was so unhappy in the Army and why hadn't he married and settled down as a gas fitter? He had thought of that once, and she could have visited him on Sundays. Then they both wondered where they'd gone wrong and longed for their Lottery number to come up so they could put it all right.

Then they had an argument about Gladys and if she should go into a home. Joy accused Carol of neglecting her mother, Old May, who spent every evening drinking in the pub and who nobody ever visited because her flat stank.

'Sometimes I'd love to put Gladys in a home, Carol, but you know as well as I do she wouldn't go. She'll probably be there when I die still putting her fag-ends down the sink and drying her knickers on the radiator.'

* * *

When Joy got home she parked round the back and crept in so Gladys wouldn't hear her and then she hung her curtains. She'd even made a little frill to go under the sink and hide the rubbish bin. She sat in a chair smoking a fag and admiring her beautiful new pale shining curtains, yellow with the green border. And then she cursed that she hadn't bought more stuff so she could have covered little cushions for the kitchen chairs to match.

Then she had another fag and, grasping this moment of peace when Gladys didn't know she was in and she wasn't out at work cleaning someone else's house, Joy took her shoes off and wandered from one room to the other. She liked the soft pile of her front-room carpet. She had bought the very best wool mix in a rich caramel brown and now four years later, fully paid up and shampooed countless times, it was still looking good as new. Hanging from the ceiling were two Italian glass chandeliers, each had ten little bulbs and the glass glittered when she lit them in the evening and the shimmer caught the beaten copper chest Jonny had brought back from holiday when his life had been hunky-dory happy and she'd hoped he was going to get engaged to Jackie.

Joy made a prawn cocktail and poured herself a glass of wine in a thin green wine glass. She had a set of six. She sat at the kitchen table looking at her curtains. She liked the glaze on the cotton. It caught the light and reflected it back off the shining white floor tiles. The flat was so quiet. She cherished her quiet time alone. She sipped her wine.

The phone rang. It was Jeff on his mobile. The van had broken down and the AA were going to be a couple of hours and he hadn't had a bite since seven and would she come down . . . he was only at the bottom of the estate?

Joy made a thermos of coffee and a couple of Marmite sandwiches and ran back down to the car. 'Fucking hell!' she had stepped right in a puddle and splashed black oily water up the leg of her best trousers. Once more she ran up the concrete stairs and changed, putting the dirty ones in a bag to give to Jeff, and belted back down the road in the little Fiat.

On the way the sky turned yellow and it started to snow. Joy shivered, she could have done without this expedition.

Jeff was looking out for her, hunched over his steering wheel, bonnet open. He jumped out, a big smile breaking across his miserable face.

'Hop in the back of the van. There's more room in there.'

So they climbed in and sat on a big pile of curtains and drank the coffee and ate the sandwiches and Jeff told her she was an angel and she told him he was going to have to get her trousers cleaned and then he gave her a cuddle and a little bit more till she told him she wasn't a teenager and he said, 'Who'd have guessed it?'

The light was dark yellow now and the air grew stiller and thicker as the snow fell in big flakes till the wide sweeping branches of the cedar tree were white. Jeff wrapped Joy in a red velvet curtain and opened the back doors of the van to keep a look-out for the rescue man and watch the snow fall across the lawns.

'Heh, what about the Fiat?' said Joy. 'I might lose sight of it.'

'Then you'll have to stay here with me for ever,' said Jeff.

'But my ears are freezing.'

And Jeff stroked a blonde curl away and then cupping his large hands he put them over her ear and blew hot air between them till she told him her ear was hot, hot, hot and then turning her face he did the other one and Joy leant against him.

'Don't go home yet.'

'Gladys is home all alone and I've been gone hours. I've got to go.'

'Stay just a little bit longer.'

'Never leave me, Jeff.'

'I'll never leave you, darling.'

GLADYS SPEAKS AGAIN

At times I feel old but most of the time I feel young. When I feel old I feel awful. I wonder what's going to become of me? Am I going to get old and graceful or am I going to get old and miserable? Now I'm eighty the life in me is going out of me and I don't want that.

I haven't got the idea of what I want to do. I want to do these things and then I don't want to do them. First I want to do them then I do them and then I think to myself: What have I done that for? It's no good moping. I try hard to make myself do my work. I dust, I hoover, although she says I don't do it properly, I do.

I would have been better off if I'd stayed single. When I got married I still had to go to work. I couldn't stay at home because I had no money. Bill never give me none. He paid the rent but as regards anything else I had to pay it. I wouldn't have had what I did have if it wasn't through the tally man. I got all my stuff off the tally man so as to make it look clean and nice. I said to Bill, 'I want so much a week off of you,' and he said, 'You won't get nothing off of me.'

I had the kiosk at Earls Court by then but he made sure it didn't last long because he put me in the family way and I nearly lost my life. I was six months pregnant when I tried to get rid of it. That was the first abortion I ever had. I didn't know what it was like. Doll done it. I thought I was going to die. They took me away in an ambulance and put me in St Stephen's Hospital and told me off. Oh I didn't half get a lecture in there. They didn't look after me like they did the other patients, the matron said, 'You know too much.' She was a bastard to me. Bill was going to put Doll away. 'I've a good mind to put that woman away,' and I said, 'You mind your own business. Nothing to do with you, that's a woman's life.'

Gracefully is slow and I think to myself: I can't do that and I can't have that but I try. I try all the time. I don't feel the same, I don't feel young no more. I feel sometimes I'm in the way. I want to go out but they may not want me and I'll be in the way.

Nobody wants your company when you're old. They want somebody young. I can't blame Teddy if he finds a younger woman. I'd let him go.

When Joy was little I'd take her everywhere with me. I'd say, 'Come on, you're coming out with me.' We'd go up the North End Road to the market.

She goes out and I wonder where she's going. She ain't asked me to go with her. Another time she'll say, 'Come on, Mum, you're coming with me.'

* * *

She's had a better life than me. She's had more comfort than what I had. I used to stay in on a Sunday so my mum could wash my clothes. My mother was clean, she never had nothing but she was clean. Very very clean. We had bare boards in our house and every one of them had to be scrubbed. They were pure white. She scrubbed them with soda. She'd take the tickings off her bed. Empty the flocks on the floor and turn them inside out and she'd wash them all.

She didn't worry about food as long as she got a sheep's head for Sunday. The rest of the time it was bread and jam.

Joy's never had to wait for food like I had to when I was a kid. She never had to do what I had to do, go out and cadge food. I used to tell them a tale, 'I haven't had nothing to eat today . . .' People used to take me in their house and give me a cup of tea and a bit of bread and jam. If I smelt some stew coming out of a door I'd say, 'That smells nice,' and she'd ask me in and give me a spoonful. I might run an errand for it. Most of the people in Holyport Road where we lived had me in their houses. When I had my tonsils out they all sent me in ice-cream.

Gladys lit a cigarette, and walked into her bedroom.

I'll tell you what, I don't like her being out, not at night. I think to myself: I hope nothing is going to happen to her. Lots of things go through my mind. You never know, do you?

I've got no friends, my friends have all gone. The only

friend I've got is Teddy and he ain't much of a friend. That's why I cling to her. I give her everything what I can.

I'd love a man if I could get hold of a nice man. If you get hold of a good one you're all right.

I've found some nice men in the Day Centre. There's one that's been a colonel in the Army. There's colonels and majors up there. That's where you meet the men, in the old folks' homes.

There's one I've had my eye on but he doesn't want me. I don't want him either, I've told him.

I'd love a young man if I could get hold of one. I'm telling you, they're not easy to find.

The nurse put this towel round me and pulled it tight and she said, 'Push down,' and as I pushed, she pulled and out came Joy.

I always wanted a girl. When I got her that was the finish. I didn't want no one else.

A woman up the top had lost her baby and she gave me this big bundle of clothes, all brand new.

I was working till a week before she was born so I bought her a new pram and someone lent me a cot to put beside the bed. I fed her at first then I had to go back to work so I weaned her. My breasts had to be bound up. Bertha bound me up. 'I'll bind you up,' she said. It was ever so tight and you couldn't take it off and it was very painful. I'd do whatever I could, go and scrub a floor for a couple of bob a week. But I never had no money. Bill never gave me none, so I said to him, 'I'm going to get a job, I can't stand this.' I found a woman to take care of the baby and I went back to work.

* * *

Joy hasn't led her life the way I wanted her to lead it. I wanted her to be high. She's had a rough life. She was only young when Jonny was born. I'd have liked her to have got on. It broke my heart when I found out she was carrying. Bill blamed me. 'It's all your fault,' he said. She was only a girl and I never used to let her out. She went round Tom's house and there was a thunderstorm. That did it. I cried, I told his mother what I thought of her. She said, 'You've got to put up with it,' very hard woman. So they got married and they took a furnished room.

The furnished room was full of bugs and I said, 'You'd better come back home,' because I never had fleas and bugs in my house, so we had her and Tom and the baby back with us. Then she wanted to go and live somewhere else so I said, 'Bleeding go!' but she soon came back again. Three times she left and came back to me.

Bill idolised little Jonny. He used to sit in the chair with him on his lap and if anybody shouted he'd go for them. He was thirty years older than me so he didn't mind sitting indoors.

I'd been at work all day. I didn't want to mind the baby. I wanted to go out with George.

Gladys walked back and forth along the walkway. She glanced through Joy's window to see if she could see her.

It's difficult when you get older and you rely on someone to come and see you and they don't come and then you don't see no one and it's very lonely and it's very upsetting too. Specially when you've been used to being surrounded by people at work and at home. That's why I keep going to the door. I go to the door and I look out and I stand on the balcony keeping a look-out for her car and I see people passing and I feel a little better. If I couldn't see people I'd go mad.

There's Mrs Bell along the other end but she's on the religious side. I want someone a bit lively and in the mood. I like a laugh. I can't go and see Daisy no more because she's ill herself.

Teddy comes up of an evening sometimes but he's got no conversation, he's just a shape in the other chair.

Everybody at the Day Centre is old-fashioned. I speak to one or two but there ain't nothing there, they're too dull. It's very hard when you look at them people. How did they come to be like that?

You have this knitting corner but you're not knitting it for yourself, you're knitting it for them. I have to put it in the sale of work. That doesn't suit me. Many times I feel young but I don't feel energetic.

I often wish I'd took up driving because I could have bought a little car and driven around the place.

I was too close to my own mother. She never used to go anywhere without me. I wasn't married a week when she had my wedding ring off my finger to put in the pawn shop. She lived with me for two years when she got old. She was mostly in bed. She had her own teeth but they were very little. She could eat as long as it was soup or stew. She took some good hidings off my dad.

Night-time's the worst. Day-time I'm all right, night-time it's lonely.

If I don't go to sleep I walk around the flat. I won't

take a sleeping pill, they're too dangerous. Sometimes I sleep in the chair all night.

Gladys stood outside on the walkway looking at Joy through her kitchen window and scratching her head.

'What are you cooking?' she called.

'Duck. It's Jeff's birthday and I'm roasting a duck.'

And Gladys went in so she could smell the roasting duck, her fag in her mouth.

'In out, in out, that's what you do.'

'When I don't go in you get the 'ump and so I stay out and you still get the 'ump.'

'Don't drop ash on my floor. I've just washed it. There'll come a time when I go back to work and you'll have to be on your own all day. I've got to keep on with my own life.'

'Here, Joy, do you remember Old Lemco? I had some capers with him.'

He made me a supervisor. It was a couple of months after Jonny was born. Joy was skeleton-thin, but her breasts were twice the size, she had so much milk. She put him in a nursery mornings and came back to work half-day with me for a while.

'Remember that duck, Joy?'

Old Lemco liked my Joy and on the Monday he's brought us in this roast duck done in greaseproof paper what he's had over from his Sunday dinner and he invites me and Joy into his office to eat it and we're sitting there tucking into this duck with our fingers. He's watching us and smoking his cigar and all the grease is running down Joy's chin, she was hungry, and he laughs, 'You were hungry,' he says, and then she laughs too and as she laughs the milk must have come sudden into her breasts and it spurts right out through her blouse and her front is all wet. She goes bright red and Old Lemco hands her his white handkerchief. I remember the way he took it from his pocket, and shook it out with a flick of his wrist, and handed it to her. I took it home and washed and ironed it and brought it back next day.

'He was nice, Old Lemco. We had some good feeds from him,' said Glad.

'Hungry, Mum?'

'I could eat a whole duck to myself. Have you made gravy?'

I don't know what I'd be like if anything ever happened to Joy. If anything happened to her I don't know what would happen to me.

THE HOLIDAY

Joy stopped on her way back from work and bought the second-hand lounger. It was blue and pale pink and looked brand spanking new. She opened it out on the balcony, poured herself a glass of iced orange and lay back bare-footed pretending she was away in some beautiful hot place with Jeff, instead of under the first spring sunshine on a council estate in South London. She kept her eyes shut so she didn't see the tower blocks casting black shadows or the acres of muddy grass strewn about with debris. Her mind went quiet. The orange tasted good. She felt the fresh air stroke her naked feet. She breathed deeply and let go of Jeff. Now she was by a green river hung about with willow trees, all alone.

Gladys wouldn't be back from the Day Centre for an hour.

Five minutes later, Joy had just dropped off, Gladys turned up.

'The bus brought me early. Look what I've got for you.'

And Gladys handed Joy a bunch of daffodils. 'They were going cheap on the corner and Eddie stopped, so I could buy them.'

I realise why I sometimes wake up in the middle of the night. I'm alone and it's quiet. I leave Jeff asleep. I make myself a cup of tea, I walk into my front room. I look at everything and I look all round and I think how I might give the room a lift. Then I turn out the light and I sit by the window looking out and I smoke a fag. Last night it was a full moon. It's the only time I ever get alone.

But I said, 'Thanks, Mum.'

It touched me, I don't ever remember her buying me flowers except on my birthday.

'I could do with a drop of orange myself,' said Gladys.

Joy got up to fetch Gladys some orange and put the daffs in water and when she came back Gladys was stretched out on the lounger.

'This is comfortable. Here, Joy, remember when we went to Spain? You and me and Carol. You got me pissed in that bar and I lost one shoe and Carol gave me odd shoes to put on and I was walking from one side to the other.'

'I was a fucker to you.'

And Gladys leant back into the cushions of the lounger and remembered Spain. They had all been sitting in deck-chairs and the sun was burning.

Sod this, I'm the only one with a top on, and I turned the chair round so nobody would see me and I took off my top, but they did see me, I caused a lot of attraction.

'You saw the bleeding people looking, didn't you, Joy, that time I took my top off? They were lovely days, they were.'

'I can see you in your brown-and-white checked costume, Mum.'

'My bookmaker's one.'

'I got you a blue-and-white one the same.'

'I never left it off.'

'Our money ran out at the end of the holiday and we met them great big blokes and they bought us dinner. Remember, Mum, I met Martin?'

'Oh fuck him. He wasn't no good. You couldn't see it. He didn't like me. I said, "You aren't taking her with you. Go on, piss off. Come on, Joy, you're coming with me." You were crying, silly cow.'

'I'd met someone and I wanted to stay behind and you wouldn't let me.'

'"You're coming home. You brought me here, you're coming home with me," that's what I said.'

Joy sat on the wicker chair beside Gladys, remembering.

She made me come home and I'll never forget it. I wanted life. I didn't want to come home. So I got drunk. I got so drunk they nearly didn't let me on the plane. I done it so I wouldn't have to get on. I was laying on the floor in the airport. I said to her, 'You're an old trollop. When you get what you want you're OK but if I want something you don't let me have it.' I sat on the plane. 'I'm sorry, Mum.' 'Don't come near me. Sorry ain't good enough,' she said. Then I cried to her. 'I didn't mean it, Mum . . . I didn't want to come home.' She hated it, she hated anyone who could take me away from her.

'Most of the blokes I've been out with, you wanted to come too. Thinking about it. You've always been there.'

'No I haven't. Pass us one of your fags, Joy. When you went to Australia with posh John you broke my heart. You didn't ought to have gone.'

'I fell in love.'

Joy leant across and lit Gladys's cigarette.

'He was no good.'

'Every bloke I've been with you'd say, "He ain't no good, he ain't no good, he ain't no good." Charlie, "He ain't no good." Ken, "He ain't no good." Mick, "He ain't no good." In the end I believe you. I think he ain't, because you believe what your mother tells you. You do believe it.'

I was in love with John, that's why I was able to run away to Australia and leave them all. She smacked John's face. She clawed all his face the night before I left. 'Don't you take my daughter away. You're no fucking good.'

I still went. I was on brandy. I was divorced. Jonny had a girlfriend. I was running the shop. It was all too much. So when John came along he was my escape.

I think Gladys is a bit of an old witch somewhere. She can always tell when something is going to go wrong. Jeff has had enough of her now. He told me Sunday, 'I've had enough of your mother, Joy.' He's got a lot of strain himself. Sometimes he's out in the van till half-past seven at night. He starts at eight, that's a long day in the traffic.

I said, 'I get tired too, Jeff, that's why I've gone off sex.'

Then he told me I should go to sleep in the afternoon for an hour and then come the time when he comes home I'd be alive. 'What about my Mum?' Then Jeff got the 'ump. He said, 'What have you got? She follows you about like a little dog. You go in the other room, she follows you. You go to the toilet and she stands outside the door.'

I hated him for saying that. He went out slamming the door and stayed the night at his mate's place. He stayed away two whole days. I couldn't eat or speak. Then he came back as if nothing had happened. I forgave him that time but I don't know what to do. I don't know what to do. When he came back he said, 'I will help you through it,' but I don't know how long I can stand it. I live fucking right next door. I turn against Jeff because I'm so angry. If I do go out on my own I'm thinking all the time: Suppose she's caught herself alight, suppose she's had a fall? Tell me what to do!

Yesterday, when I came back from work, it was a beautiful evening. I saw Gladys come out on to the balcony as I parked my car. Six geese, in formation, flew overhead, cackling, on their way across the spread-out sky above the tall flats. She is looking out for me but the light is too dim for her to see me wave. I see her white head and pale face as she peers over the balcony railing. I call to her as I get out of my car. 'It's me. I'm back!'

'I thought it was you,' she shouts down and I guess she's been peering over at every car hoping each time it was me but never really having a clue. She won't wear her new glasses and she can see fuck all through the old ones. The shadow of the water tower was black on the sunlit wall, the evening sun was just about to disappear.

An aeroplane flew over. A dog barked and Gladys hurried down the concrete ramp to meet me, hanging on to the rail so as not to lose her balance.

That's my life.

'Have you had a row with Jeff? He's not talking. Is it me keep coming in?'

'No, Mum.'

'I don't like that car. I'm frightened you'll have an accident in it.'

'Don't leave no fag-ends on my balcony. Use the ashtray.'

'I wish I could see George, he must be dead by now. I don't know if Bert's died or not.'

'No, you spoke to Bert the bus driver on the phone last week. I got through for you.'

'They don't tell you what they die of. You just find out they're dead.'

'George died.'

'Oh George died.'

'Arthur died.'

'Two Arthurs died.'

'Two Arthurs. Johnnie the brick.'

'Yes, Johnnie the brick, all cancer and drink. I've had five lovers that I can remember, and they're all five dead. Only one left me some money. Arthur left me two hundred pounds. His family didn't like it. Too bad. I went with George for ten years. I met him on a bus. Oh no, it was in the pub. It was home time and he offered me a drink. "You've asked me now when it's time to go home. You didn't ask me before, did you?"

'I was saucy to him. They like a bit of sauce. We walked round to a little alleyway and we had five minutes against the wall. I went with him for ten years after that. I went away on holidays. Went away Christmas.'

'He took you away to Jersey, didn't he, and paid for me to come too?'

'Yes, we went to Jersey, we did.'

'Me and you went to Jersey. Jonny, he was only young then, came too.'

'Yes, we went on ahead. I didn't want my Bill to find out. But he found out in the end. "You and your fucking George. Wait till I get hold of him."'

'It was the first time I'd ever flown. Tom had just got ten years.'

'He only paid for you because he wanted to take me. Get me a drop more brandy, Joy.'

'We stayed in the Sunshine Hotel.'

'The Blue Star Hotel.'

'Oh the Blue Star, I thought it was the Sunshine Hotel.'

'Sunshine Hotel, that's right.'

'Thought it was,' said Joy.

'Then you got off with the manager.'

'I've got some lovely photos of Jersey somewhere, Mum.'

'I minded little Jonny while you went out with the manager. I said, "Don't make it late." And you come in at three in the morning.'

'I was smoking all those beautiful cigarettes with the colours, wasn't I?'

'Continental cigarettes,' said Gladys. 'Sobranies . . . all pinks and blues. Go with all your dresses.'

'There were black ones with gold tips.'

'They were Turkish cigarettes. I brought forty home with me. I took them to work. I was working at the baths then. I should have stayed there.'

'That's years ago, Mum. Hasn't it gone quick?'

'I would have had a nice pension. But no, I wanted to get away. I thought I could find something better.'

'Not only that. It was too damp with the soap getting down your throat,' said Joy.

'Yes, it caused a lot of chest problems.'

Gladys shut her eyes. She thought again of Arthur.

'Arthur was the one with a bit of money. I loved him.'

'You loved him and he loved you.'

'We loved one another.'

'It was a happy time,' said Joy.

'He give you your fare to get home from Australia that time you were stranded.'

'Yeah, he gave me my fare home.'

'He did it for my sake.'

'He was a very kind fellow,' said Joy.

'Then he got cancer. They opened him up and he was dead in the four weeks. It was the gaiety life that killed him. I've got some good memories of him.'

Gladys went and filled the glasses and when she came back Joy was on the lounger.

'You can have it again in five minutes, Mum, I've got to go to the post office and get your pension.'

'My hair started falling out soon after he died. I'd had a

perm for the funeral. I went round to see her, the woman who done the perm, and she gave me some money to keep my mouth shut but I never went again for a long time. When I went again I said, "I hope it doesn't fall out this time." "No," she said, "it must have been you. You must have been ill." Here, take a look, Joy, it's itching again.'

'That was years ago, Mum. You had too many perms. Come here, I'm sitting down.'

Gladys bent her head and Joy put her glasses on and parted Glad's sparse hair with her fingers.

'Nothing there, Mum.'

'I've seen her since but I won't speak to her. She put lacquer on it and turned it orange.'

'I'm going to wash it for you tonight,' said Joy.

Gladys sat down satisfied. 'It looks nice and white when I wash it with that Swedish expensive shampoo. I was going to keep it for myself.'

Gladys sat beside Joy and listened to four or five blackbirds singing in the lime trees, singing as if their hearts would burst and melt with song.

'Got anything to eat? It's very nice out here.'

'In a minute, Mum.'

So sat Joy and Gladys drinking their tea on the balcony by the window boxes stuffed with purple and yellow pansies. The air was soft with the smell of spring and still the blackbirds sang.

Joy got to her feet. 'I'm going to the post office.'

'What for?'

'To fetch your pension. I need some money.'

'What have I got to give you the money for?'

'You've got to give me forty-four pounds, that's for me. That's my attendance allowance,' said Joy.

'I don't need nothing.'

'And ten pounds for your fags.'

'I don't smoke that much.'

'You do, Mum. You have twenty fags a day.'

'I don't. Twenty fags lasts me three days.'

'Well, how come you haven't got any?'

'He's nicked them.'

'Ted wouldn't touch your fags, he's got his own. No, don't touch mine.'

'I'll come with you,' said Gladys.

'Come on then, we'll stroll over.'

Gladys combed her hair.

'I look fat in these.'

If she wears trousers she tucks everything inside. Her petticoat, her corset, and then she wonders why she looks fat.

'You've got to change that cardigan! I won't have tea stains or fag burns. I can't handle it.'

'Oh sod it, it's all right!'

'I'm not taking you out like that. Change it!' said Joy. 'And give your face a wash when you come back from the Day Centre and put your teeth in Steradent.'

'I'm not wasting my money on Steradent.'

My poor Mum with her teeth. They're getting too big for her and she dribbles and she doesn't talk right and now her petticoat is hanging down the back of her trousers. I got her a new petticoat to wear under the two new dresses I bought her but she's gone back indoors and put on her old faithful with all the fag burns down the front. I bought her this beautiful new dress, it's blue and matches her eyes, but she won't wear it. Says it's too long and I can't be bothered to take it up.

'Come on, I haven't got time to hang about.'

'You were stretched on that lounger half asleep when I came in.'

'I'd cleaned a great big house, Mum.'

'Don't moan, I went to work till I was seventy years old.'

They walked along beside the red-brick wall, along the backs of the Parade shops. Delivery vans were parked up on the pavement so they had to walk in the road, sprinkled with broken glass and wet cardboard boxes. Beards of dandelions flew about, fluff in the breeze. Four Red Admirals were perched on a scruffy buddleia growing out of the bricks. A brown dog stood howling in the road.

'Give him a biscuit, Joy.'

'I haven't got a biscuit.'

'Here, there's a sweet in my bag.'

She scrambled in the bottom of her bag while Joy waited and, finding a lemon drop, threw it to the dog who, after a quick sniff, picked it up and made off with it.

'I knew he was hungry.'

Bricks lay about and some battered thistles grew by the giant dustbins and bits of paper fluttered and were caught in the brambles among last year's shrivelled dusty blackberries.

'Look out for the bee, Mum!'

'He can smell my perfume. My leg aches, go slower.'

'We'll miss the post office if you go much slower.'

I'm supposed to be taking Gladys back to the doctor tomorrow for the results of her heart. I should be taking her water every day but I haven't taken it. It's a waste of time. When she wants sugar she has it.

A spider's web hung from an oak tree. Two silver threads anchored it to a branch above and two to the grass below. A tiny hopeful spider sat in the middle. A yellow butterfly settled on a wild mallow.

The counter was at the back of the newsagent's. The queue was so long it came right out on to the pavement and when it was their turn to go inside Gladys nearly tripped over a doll's pram parked in the doorway and was within an inch of falling head over heels.

'Hold up, Mum!'

They squeezed past racks of cards, MUM, GRANDDAD, NANNY, WIFE, GOLDEN ANNIVERSARY. Women with pushchairs crowded out the queue. Gladys handed in the book and the nice fat notes were counted out.

They walked back down the road and stopped to talk to Eileen and Bev and their mother Ivy, tottering along.

'We found Mum on the floor last night. She couldn't get up,' said Eileen.

'Tell Gladys how long you had been down on the floor, Mum,' said Bev.

'I went down towards the end of *Neighbours*,' said Ivy.

'We knew then, she'd only laid there for forty-five minutes,' said Bev.

'Couldn't get up, Gladys,' said Ivy. 'I tried but I couldn't make it, I had to wait,' and she laughed. 'It was funny really, Joy.'

'She didn't mind,' said Eileen. 'She hadn't caught cold and she knew we'd be back before long.'

'Nice people,' said Joy when they'd walked on a little way.

'They're not my kind of people. I couldn't hear what they were saying. I like a bit of sport, I do. This ain't life, is it?' said Gladys.

And Joy only sighed.

'You can start wearing your little deaf-aid indoors.'

'I'm not wearing that, it makes me look old.'

'Only indoors. You don't have to wear it out. At least you could hear the bell when you're on your own.'

They went indoors to Gladys's and put the kettle on.

'Now come here, Mum.' Joy got the hearing-aid out of its box. 'These cost three hundred pounds, you know, if you buy them private. You're lucky, they gave you this one free.'

Joy put Gladys's hearing-aid in very carefully.

'Fuck me, I can hear what I'm saying now.'

'I told you.'

'It's making a terrible hissing noise!'

'That's the kettle.'

'I don't like it. I'm taking it out.'

'Leave it in, Mum. Save me shouting.'

'I don't like it. Take it out, Joy.'

Joy took it out.

Gladys counted her money every night. She's got a jar full of coins and she counts them every night. She got them out on the kitchen table and put them in piles.

'Someone's nicked my money and I think it's Teddy.'

'No, you've lost it.'

'Ted's had it. I told you he was no good.'

'No, Mum, he ain't had it. Where've you put it? Give me the money for your fags.'

Joy got out the brown envelopes and set the money aside as she did every week. Council tax, rent, TV licence, telephone, gas, electricity, cigarettes.

She has her hundred cigarettes a week. So that's her whole pay out before she starts. That comes to fifty-six pounds, fifty-six pence for them bits, her essentials, before she starts on her food. Forty-four pounds is for me, and then whatever she has over goes in there. All the odd money goes in there, so if she needs new shoes or glasses that comes out of there. She's terrific with money, she knows what's going on when it comes to money.

Teddy turned up and stood in the corner rubbing at his rheumy eye. He'd brought a packet of fags for Gladys. Ted was going into hospital in a week or two for an op on his varicose veins. They had been troubling him rather worse of late but he was frightened of going into hospital and frightened at the thought of an operation.

'Will you be able to pop over and feed the cat, Joy? She belonged to Mother and I couldn't see nothing happen to her.'

'I'll feed her for you, Teddy, don't you worry.'

Jeff came home early. It was spring and he hoped to surprise Joy with a bunch of flowers. He planned to seduce her with his big bunch of white tulips and a fillet of beef. It seemed weeks she'd been off sex. She'd even locked the mask away. He went into the flat. He knew she was next door, it was pension day and she'd be in in a moment.

He washed his hands and face. Then he put the kettle on and waited. When she came in he jumped to his feet and handed her the flowers.

'I've got best fillet for dinner.' He pointed to the bloody parcel on the table.

'Thanks, Jeff,' said Joy.

'Come to bed.'

'I can't.'

'It's been weeks.'

'I don't care if it's been months. I hate my life.'

JONNY COMES HOME

Jeff left for work and Joy, still in her dressing gown, tidied up breakfast. She was tired, they'd stayed up watching the midnight movie and then they'd drunk a couple of bottles of lager, Joy lying stretched out on the sofa, her feet in Jeff's lap. Finally after much persuasion they'd made love so it had been a short night.

There was a long ring on the downstairs bell. She picked up the intercom.

'Military Police. Can we come up?'

Two of them came up the stairs. Joy was standing in the door shaking.

'Mrs Steadman?'

'Yes.'

'Your son's gone missing. Is he here?'

'No!'

'He's done a runner. Done a bunk.'

'He's deserted. It's a very serious offence,' said the second one in case she hadn't understood.

Joy, white with shock and trembling, let them search the flat.

'Do you know where he might be?'

'No. No. No.'

'Well, get in touch with this number when he turns up,' and they were gone calling over their shoulders as they went. 'Remember, he's done a bunk, Mrs Steadman. He's done a runner. He's a deserter. It's a very serious offence. Get in touch immediately. Don't delay.'

And they were gone.

She rang Jeff on his mobile.

'Come home. Jonny's gone missing.'

Jeff headed for home, his rails full of clean, waiting to be delivered, garments swinging wildly on the corners.

He found Joy retching in the sink. Jeff poured her a glass of water and wiped her face with a damp flannel. He held her in his arms and then made her strong sweet tea and helped her put her clothes on.

'Sit on the bed, I'll put your socks on for you.'

Gladys came in and seeing Jeff home said, 'Haven't you gone to work? What's the matter with her?'

'Just leave us alone, Glad, till she's dressed, and I'll give you a shout.'

Gladys stood in the bedroom doorway, fag in mouth.

'What's the matter with you then?'

'Jonny's gone missing from the Army, Mum.'

'I told you he should never have joined the Army. Too soft. He'll turn up here. Don't you worry!'

'Go and have your breakfast, Mum. I'll be in in a moment.'

But Gladys still stood there, the ash on her cigarette

growing longer till it dropped off on to Joy's pride-of-long white bedroom carpet. Jeff gently eased Joy's sweater over her head and combed back the hair out of her eyes.

'He can get six months for this, you know. He can't take the Army so I can't see him taking to prison,' said Gladys, drawing hard on her fag. 'Six months, that's what Jack got when he deserted in peacetime. It's worse if you desert when there's a war on.'

And Joy cried some more. Then the bus came for Gladys and Jeff found her coat and Eddie said she could have breakfast when she got to the Centre, he couldn't wait any longer.

When she'd gone Jeff sat down in the armchair and took Joy on his lap and she sobbed.

'S'posin' he comes home while I'm out, Jeff. I can't go to work.'

'Carry on as usual, love. Whatever's going to happen will all happen if you go to work or not. Besides, you can't just sit here waiting.'

So they both went to work. Luckily it was Mrs Holtby's day and she told Joy she looked terrible and she was to skip the work this morning and she would make her tea and toast, she could make up the work another day, and they sat together and Joy told Mrs Holtby she was worried Jeff couldn't take much more.

'But I'm not Almighty God, Mrs Holtby, and I'm not even Almighty when it comes to my mother and my son.'

And Jonny was a man now. She knew that he would have to find his own Kingdom of Heaven, as she, at rare moments, had found hers. But she was sick with fear.

* * *

When Joy got home lunchtime she found Jonny behind the giant dustbin waiting for her.

'Oh Jonny, whatever happened?'

Joy wept to see his dirty clothes, his uncombed hair, his miserable eyes.

'I couldn't handle it any longer, Mum.'

'You'd better come in and have a cup of tea.'

Joy found him some of Jeff's clean clothes to put on and Jeff's razor so he could have a shave. He had a bath and Joy cooked him a meal and while he ate she said, 'Now you'd better phone and tell them you're here and face the music.'

But Jonny begged and pleaded.

'Just one night at home. Please, Mum, please.'

When Jeff came back Jonny was asleep on the sofa so they had to sit in the kitchen and there wasn't much for dinner because Jonny had eaten it.

'You'd better let the authorities know tomorrow, Joy, or you'll be in trouble for harbouring,' said Jeff.

'Harbouring my own son?' said Joy, and then she shut up for fear of causing a row.

Her heart sank like a stone. She couldn't even cry any more. She cooked Jeff eggs and bacon. He sat in silence doing the crossword.

When Gladys came home from the Day Centre she took one look at Jonny asleep and said, 'Well, he's home and it doesn't look as if he's going anywhere. I told you the Army wouldn't suit him.'

And she stood by Jeff's chair letting off wind.

Jeff was more than fed up, he was angry. Angry on his own behalf, angry on Joy's. It wasn't much fun sitting up on the slippery plastic chairs in the kitchen so they went to bed early and Jeff wanted to make love but Joy wouldn't let him touch her, not even for a cuddle.

In the night Jonny woke and tuned in to some late-night station and turned up the music. And this went on for days and each day Joy would say, 'Please, Jonny, make that phone call.'

The first week turned into the second week and Jonny hadn't been out of the flat and each day he begged his mother for one more night and each night, Jeff coming back from work would find him there, the music turned full volume, and he would row with Joy shouting at her to make that phone call, calling her a rotten mother who couldn't make her son do the right thing and each day Gladys coming home from the Day Centre would say, 'He still here? He should be back in the Army. It's not Christmas, you know, Jonny.' But some days Gladys felt sorry for him and invited him in to watch the racing with her and Teddy. And sometimes the three of them would have a game of cards.

'Like a cup of tea, Nan?' said Jonny. 'How about you, Ted?'

He was more relaxed in here, nobody shouted at him.

But Joy's misery mounted higher and higher and Jeff came home later and later and his face was black as thunder.

'You need someone with money,' said Jeff. 'I'm not going to give you no more just to give to them. When I bring meat home you cook it for them. They eat it!'

'You eat it too.'

'Yes, I eat it too, but I bought it.'

Gladys came in.

'Take a look,' she said, bending towards Joy.

'No, I'm not looking in your hair no more, Mum, I'm fed up with your hair.'

'Don't then! Don't bother about me! You don't care about me! I'm your mother, you should look after me!'

'I do look after you. What do you think is in that drawer there? Brand-new glasses, you never wear them. Your brand-new hearing-aid is in the drawer, you won't put that in, and your brand-new dentures which I got done for you.' Joy was fighting her tears and her rage. 'I've got to get away from here.'

'You're always out anyway!' said Gladys, angry too.

Jeff had gone into the bedroom and turned on the telly. Now the music was going in the front room and the telly in the bedroom.

'Put that fag in the ashtray, I'll put you in a home if you catch my place alight. I'm not having it!'

'This is my house. I'll do what I want here!'

'This is my flat, Mum.'

'Well, you're my daughter, aren't you? Leave off shouting.'

And in her despair Joy asked herself what could she do about anything? She felt less and less in control of her life.

Things were going badly at work for Jeff. The boss had intimated he was slow with deliveries. There had been a complaint of rudeness from a customer and two wrong deliveries the day before and unless . . . Jeff knew it was because he was getting no sleep and rowing with Jonny and screaming at Joy and after two weeks of this he hated everyone including his boss and his customers.

That evening he escaped to the bath hardly speaking to Joy as he came through the door. He was lying there, his eyes shut, Joy's pink flannel across his forehead, Jonny's music was pounding through the sitting-room wall, when the bathroom door had opened and Gladys came in, pulled down her knickers and sat down on the toilet. Then she saw Jeff.

'You having a bath, Jeff?'

And Jeff jumped out of the bath and ran wet and naked into the kitchen where Joy was cooking the dinner.

'I can't stand this any longer! Get rid of both of them or I go.'

'How can I, Jeff? How can I? Tell me how!'

JEFF LEAVES

Joy moved about the kitchen cooking the dinner. Stretching the stew to feed Gladys, Jeff, herself and Jonny.

From behind the closed door of the sitting room loud music thundered. The heavy beat tore at her nerves. She opened the door. Jonny was stretched on the sofa.

'Please turn it down!'

She shouted really loud to make him hear, gesturing with her hand at the same time.

He leant and turned down the volume knob.

'Mum, it's all I've got, my music.'

She left the room and shut the door. Her heart was full of dread. Then Jeff came in and as she turned to greet him, 'Hello, love,' she caught his face, all tight and solemn, and she knew something was coming.

'Joy, I've got to talk to you.'

'Can't it wait till after dinner, Jeff?'

'No, I'm not staying for dinner. I've got to go. I've got to sort myself out.'

'What are you saying?'

'I can't handle it. I can't think in this house. I've got to get away. Barry at work has moved in with his girlfriend. I can have his flat.'

'You never told me you was thinking of moving out! You never said nothing!'

She caught hold of his jacket.

'I'm fed up with this life. I can't go on like this.' Jeff turned his face away and cried and Joy pressed against him crying too. 'Listen to him!' Jonny had turned up the volume again and the walls vibrated with the deadening monotonous beat. 'I'm leaving you because I can't take it any more.' He tried to push Joy away but she clung on. 'I get no peace, no peace at all. I've got to get out of here.'

Joy choking on her sobs couldn't speak.

'I feel used. I'm an old Joe on the side. All the money we saved for our holiday you've spent on Jonny.'

'He had nothing, Jeff.'

'I don't want to live like this.'

'I've got to let him stay here till they find him. He's got nowhere else to go. I thought we were in this together, when you loved someone you faced things together!'

'Let him get his own place.'

'I'd never have rested if I hadn't taken him in.'

'Rested! What kind of rest is this? I've been at work all day.'

And Joy let go of Jeff. She couldn't explain the vastness of the fear you feel for your son when his world has broken apart and everything has fallen to pieces and you know his desolation.

'He's in bad bad trouble, Jeff. He's screwed up his life. If he wants to stay with me he can.'

Jeff turned away.

'I always come last with you, Joy.'

'What about me? I left my job and I go cleaning to make the money stretch.'

'Yes, to feed your grown-up son.'

'All right, to feed him, and so I've got to. I've got to try and help him survive. It's all I know how to do.'

'I've got to go, Joy.'

Joy's voice went low.

'I can't beg you to stay.'

She felt nothing save a vague numbness and a great weight in her limbs as if they were too heavy to move. And Jeff bent towards her to hear. And then he moved away and went over to the window.

'I'll fetch my stuff when you're out at work.'

'I can't even make you any promises that things will change here but . . .'

'I'm leaving you!'

And he opened the door.

Then Joy broke. She heard her voice shrieking from a long way off. Saying things she never meant to say.

'I love you. Please don't leave me.'

And Jeff was shouting too. Shouting loud above the noise of the thundering music.

'I love you, Joy, but I've got to get out of here.'

But he found her in his arms.

'Do you think I want to spend my time picking dog-ends

out of the sink?' She clung to him. 'I want to get into a Range Rover beside you with my dark glasses on and drive away from all this. But I can't, I can't get away from it!'

Jeff pushed her hard and ran out of the house. Joy ran to the sink and was sick. She fell down on her knees and then prostrate on her face and turning her head from side to side and crying out she rubbed her cheeks on the door mat, red raw, till they bled.

She sobbed for an hour, her body heaving, while in the room next door Jonny had once again turned up the volume of his music to giant decibels, deaf to his mother and her sobs.

Then Gladys home from the Day Centre walked in and found the stew burnt and Joy face-downwards on the floor.

'Whatever happened to you? Where's Jeff?'

The next day Joy spent all day in bed when she wasn't in the bathroom bathing her face.

I hated Jeff for going. I looked on him as a husband, not a boyfriend, and I thought: Well, fuck you. I put up with a lot from him. I can't help it if Jonny's here. It won't be for long and as for Mum, what can I do?

And Gladys made her a cup of tea and she drank it and Jonny woke up and came and sat in the kitchen and they each had a fag.

What if this goes on for ten years? But I'm petrified of her going into a home. Petrified. I couldn't handle it. I couldn't do it. They wouldn't know how to look after her same as I do.

* * *

As soon as her face was down Joy went back to work.

One day soon after, while Jonny was still asleep and Joy was at work, Jeff collected all his clothes, all his bits and all his pieces, and loaded them into the dry-cleaning van and took them to his mate's house.

Joy wondered how she'd pay the bills without Jeff. The telephone and the electric were due in this month. However would she pay them without him? She felt racked and ruined. She cleaned the Executive's house from top to bottom.

GETTING THE WALLPAPER

It's Friday and I'm taking Gladys to Texas to buy some wallpaper to do her bedroom.

Fuck Jeff, I'll do it for her myself.

We get in the car. I like to get in and it starts. Well, it won't start. I try again. Nothing. Now I've got Mum and me in the car, the battery is flat and I've got to push it down the ramp and it's raining. It's useless asking Jonny because he's still asleep on the settee and if I wake him up he'll take hours getting dressed and then he won't want to come out in case someone sees him.

'I'll help you push it,' said Gladys opening the door.

'Sit in the fucking car!'

I'm angry now. I'm nearly breaking my back pushing the car with her in it. And that's when I really need a man. I need Jeff when my car goes wrong. Now the car is running down the ramp. I'm panicky. Suppose it runs away with her in it? I jump in and thank Christ it starts up and we're on our way.

We got to Texas and she looked at all the papers. First she wanted one.

'This'll go with my duvet cover.'

And then she wanted another.

'I've always liked lemon, haven't I? What do you think, Joy?'

And it took hours and I wasn't in the mood.

At last she chose the paper she wanted, little mauve pansies and the border all lilac and green. We had an argument about how many rolls she needed and there was a long wait to pay.

When we came out I'd had enough. We got back into the car and it didn't feel right, it was wonky. I got out and looked, one of the tyres was very low, it had a slow puncture. So when I get to the petrol station I go over to the AIR and I say to Mum, 'Fuck, we need ten pence.' And I've gone to look in my bag and my purse is gone.

'I had fifteen pounds in there and that's every penny I've got.' I shouted at her, 'It's you, you fucking want everything done. You want this, you want that. I'm sick to death of it!'

'It'll be all right. Just put ten pence in it.'

'Well, give me ten pence.'

I'm sitting on the ground in my best white trousers trying to put the air in. I'm dirty now and I hate those valves. I need a man by my side.

'Is it all right now?' she says as if fuck all has happened.

I spot my purse underneath the seat.

'I've found my purse!'

'I knew you never left it in there.'

As if she knew fuck all about it. Now she wants to go to ASDA.

'Now look, before we go in I've only got fifteen quid. Do NOT pick loads of gear up, Mum.'

'Don't shout.'

Anyway, in we went and Gladys took out her purse and she's got a twenty in there and a five in another pocket.

'What are you doing with all that money?'

'It's my money.'

Now we're going round ASDA's and she's picking up this and she's picking up that and I'm thinking about what my mates have been saying. The girls have been telling me how to cut down on expenses.

Carol's first, 'I don't have no lighting on, don't have no heating on. Put a blanket round you to watch telly of an evening.'

Then there's Peggy saying, 'Go to Sainsbury's and buy four pies for two pounds, you can have one of them every day. Make yourself beans on toast the other days.'

I sat there and I said, 'If I've got to live like that I'll go out whoring.'

'Times are different,' Carol said. 'You haven't got a bloke on your side now.'

'No, maybe I haven't, but I don't fucking need a bloke to put a bit of grub on my table.'

I was wild.

'You don't really need that, Mum.'

'I know what I want.'

'Do you fancy a cup of tea?'

'Yes.'

'I'm going to cook you liver and bacon tonight and

I've got a box of new potatoes, we'll have those. Leave the trolley there then and sit at a table and I'll go get us a cup.'

I come back with the tea and she's got the trolley right in the aisle beside her so no one can get past.

'What did you bring that in for?'

'She's got one over there. That Jeff, he's looking for someone with money. He doesn't want you because you've got nothing.'

'Oh shut up, Mum.'

'I want to go to the toilet, where is it?'

'Over there and take that fag out of your mouth, you can't take that with you.'

At last we're in the car, we're on our way to the boot sale where I'm meeting Carol and Peggy. All of a sudden she's caught short.

'I want to go to the toilet.'

'Not again.'

It is packed down Putney High Street. Jam-packed.

'Pull up here. I'll go in the pub.'

I've pulled up and I've got everybody screaming and beeping their hooters. People coming out of Sainsbury's can't get past.

She came out and she's got toilet on her coat. I knew she'd never make it.

'Mum, I'm taking you home.'

SHE SHOUTED REALLY LOUD, 'You take me home! That'll be your lot!'

She pointed her finger at me and I nearly ran into the car in front. She was spitting on her handkerchief and wiping at her coat, she didn't even notice we'd nearly had an accident.

'Whether you like it or not I'm taking you home. You cannot go to the boot sale if you've got a bad stomach.'

'You fucking ain't leaving me behind. That's all you want to do is push me away from it all. Your pride will put you in a box.'

I took her back home.

'You've got to have a wash and change your clothes. I'll wait.'

'Fucking hell. I don't know what's the matter with you.'

She wiped at her coat again.

'You go in the bathroom and wash yourself. You stink.'

'Oh you're too fussy, you get on my fucking nerves. Why did Jeff leave?'

'Because you kept coming in all the time.'

'I'm never in there. Never!'

'Yes you are. You're always in my place.'

'No I'm not. I just walk in and walk out.'

'Yeah, you put your fucking ash on my floor. You stand there passing wind.'

'No I don't.' Then all of sudden she went like a little girl. 'You're not leaving me?'

'No, Mum.'

Anyway she changed her clothes and off we go again. We got to the boot sale. I can't see Carol or Peg anywhere. They must have got fed up waiting. Then I spotted this great big leopard for two pounds.

'I'm having that.'

'I want that dog,' said Gladys.

'Well, I saw it first. It's a leopard. It ain't a dog.'

'Well, I'm having it. It'll look nice on my bed. It'll set it off.'

'It'll look better on my bed among the lace pillows. Your bed is too old-fashioned.'

'You want everything,' said Gladys.

'I bought you that nice green candlewick bedspread. Fitted. That'll do you,' I said, fishing in my purse for two pounds.

'My legs ache,' said Glad.

'I told you you can't walk about.'

'I can. I'm hungry.'

They went to the pie-and-mash shop. Gladys took the sugar packets off the table and put them in her bag.

'You're not allowed sugar,' said Joy.

'Mind your own business.'

They tucked in to hot pie and mash and thick green liquor. Glad had two eels too.

'Here, you know what?' she says to two fellows at the same table. They go on eating. 'I came in here when I was five years old. It was my birthday and I danced on that table over there.'

'Did you, love?'

The young fellow smiled at his mate who smiled back. They went on eating.

'You finished, Mum?'

When they got outside Gladys said, 'They took the piss. Nobody wanted to know.'

'Oh never mind.'

And then Joy saw a man hanging about, a good-looking guy. Suddenly a woman ran across the street and he caught her in his arms. And Joy's heart was shot white hot, so much did she long for Jeff.

'Hurry up, Mum.'

She helped Glad into the car.

'Where are we going now?'

'We're going home.'

'I'm going to find myself another bloke.'

'Mum, I'd have thought you'd have had enough of blokes in your lifetime.'

'Why did Jeff leave? It wasn't anything to do with me coming in, was it?'

'It was you and Jonny and the whole bleeding lot.'

'Me!'

'Yes, he got fed up with you always coming in.'

'I didn't come in much when he was in there.'

'Yes, you did. You was always in there.'

'Well, I came in to see if you were in. I didn't fucking interfere with him.'

'He didn't want me looking after you.'

'What! It's your duty to look after me. All daughters look after their mothers.'

'Yeah, Mum, but you can't have all my life.'

'I'm no trouble to you. If you don't want to look after me, don't look after me but you're not going to put me in a home.'

'I'd never put you in a home. I'd die before that and I most probably will die before you the way things are going.'

'Well, if you died I'd die with you.'

When they got home Gladys tried to carry the heavy

shopping so Joy wouldn't have to make two journeys up the stairs.

'Here, I'll take this lot.'

She was puffing and blowing.

'It's too heavy for you, Mum.'

'No, I'll carry it, Joy. I really like coming out with you. I enjoy myself. We had a nice day today, didn't we?'

We'd only been out for a couple of hours and I'd been a miserable cow. It broke my heart.

Well, when I got indoors I had a large brandy and coffee. I had to. Jonny was still in bed with his music going. I hated Jeff for leaving me. I could have torn him apart.

Later that afternoon I took Gladys up the clinic for her fortnightly check-up. I didn't want to, it was one of those days when everything was on top of me.

The nurse said, 'Your mother's sugar is very high. I want you to test it four times a day, blood twice and urine twice.'

The doctor said, 'I want her blood taken three times a day and her urine,' and I thought: I can't do all this, I can't take any more.

We came home and I looked at her. She's stood there scratching her head and I thought: I can't do it. I don't want no more. I don't want no fucking more. I couldn't handle it. I was frantic. She went back in her own house to see Teddy and my brain went and I thought: Oh fuck it, I'll have a drink. This must have been about four o'clock, I had a glass of wine and then another and then another, till I finished the bottle off and then I was getting the flavour. I went next door to Gladys.

Gladys, Teddy and Jonny sat in a row watching the racing on telly and smoking. Teddy had been across to the betting shop and placed three bets. Jonny got up and walked up and down.

'Hello, Joy,' said Ted.

'Hello, Ted,' said Joy. 'Would you like a drink?'

'Yes, I will if you don't mind,' said Ted, glancing apprehensively at Gladys and licking his lips.

'Keep quiet, Joy,' said Gladys. 'What's the matter with you, Jonny? Sit down, they're under starter's orders!'

Gladys leant closer to the telly. Teddy was beside her, he loosened his collar and ran his tongue around his gums. Jonny still paced the room.

Joy found a bottle of port in Gladys's bar and poured herself and Teddy a drink.

'Cheers,' he said winking at her, his head back so Gladys didn't see.

'You've been drinking,' said Gladys looking up. 'You won't be able to drink in the hospital, Teddy. Oh, I may as well have one to keep you company.'

Jonny had one too. He knocked it back in one swallow and continued pacing while Joy poured herself another glass of port.

And even when the race began Jonny found it hard to sit down and watch, with pleasure, the beautiful horses, sleek and sweating necks straining hell for leather along the bright-green turf. Even racehorses couldn't reach him. He went on pacing, turning his head sideways towards the telly and drawing on his fag.

Meanwhile Joy went on drinking and when the port was gone she found half a bottle of Bailey's and drank that and then she went back in her house and phoned everybody she could think of and told them what she thought of them.

Then she came back and started in on Gladys.

'You drain me. You brainwash me.'

'You should look after me. I looked after my mother.'

And then she turned on Jonny.

'As for you!'

'Leave him alone,' said Gladys, 'he's never been right since he fell out of that tree when he was seven. You should never have let him go in the Army.'

'How could I stop him? He was a grown man.'

'Leave him alone, he can sleep in with me. You shouldn't drink.'

'I'll drink what I like, I don't want you round me all the time telling me what to do. I want my own life. You've had yours.'

'I don't know what you're talking about. I'm your mother. I'm no nuisance to you.'

'My whole life is wrapped round you and if anything happens to you I'll be lost.'

'I don't know what you're fucking on about,' said Gladys.

Then Joy opened Gladys's cupboard and got out all her tins of peaches-in-syrup and chucked them in the bin.

'You leave my stuff alone,' Glad shouted.

'I don't want you to take my life away.' Tears shot out

of Joy's eyes. 'What is my life with Jeff gone? I wish I was dead.'

Gladys poured them both a drink.

'Never mind, love. Have a drink.'

Teddy scratched his stubbly chin and stared hard at the telly.

Several drinks and a few races later Joy toppled and fell. Jonny and Teddy picked her up off the floor and carried her next door to her own bed. When they'd gone Gladys took her shoes off and covered her over.

Getting drunk eased the pain. I got my frustration out. It took me three days to get over it. It was all that testing they wanted me to do on Gladys, all the responsibility, that's what set me off. Afterwards I thought: It's so little to do and it is for your mother, but at the time I couldn't.

GOODBYE, JONNY

It was Sunday again. Jonny had folded up his bedclothes and put them neatly at the end of the settee. Now he sat at the kitchen table, smoking Joy's last fag and staring into space. Gladys stood in the doorway scratching her head. Joy washed up the breakfast.

'Teddy's cooking dinner for you today. I'm going to drop you there later, Mum.'

'I'm not going.'

'He's got chuck steak and carrots and onions.'

'I'm not going.'

'He's expecting you. He's going to make dumplings.'

'I'm not going.'

'You've got to go. He's going into hospital tomorrow and he's worried about the cat.'

'He's going to put something in the dinner to poison me.'

'Well, I'm going out.'

'I'm coming with you.'

'No you're not. I'm going on my own,' said Joy.

Gladys stomped up and down the walkway, her face was grim. She was in a rage. She stood in the doorway.

'I'm not going to Teddy's. It's cold there.'

'You can wear your warm coat.'

'He won't cook a proper dinner.'

'You won't starve.'

Gladys turned her back and stared out of the window.

Jonny stood up tossing his cigarette into the bin.

'I'm going to have a shower, Mum.'

'You had one last night. I can't afford it, Jonny.'

And without a word he went into the front room and turned on the music very very loud so the endless pulsating beat went in one side of Joy's head and out the other. She followed him and turned off the music.

'No, Jonny, I'm not having it. Not when I'm in.'

'My head's going all over the place.'

'Now stop! The only reason your head's going all over the place is because you're bored. That's what's the matter with you.'

'You don't listen!'

'I don't want to listen any more, Jonny. You've made all your mistakes, now you've got to get out of this mess. There's the phone!'

'I can't.'

'You've got to make a move and start looking after yourself.'

'I can't make that call.'

'But you fucked it up. You ran away. You should have told your CO you wasn't happy, that you needed to visit your family. You fucked up and now you've got to pay for it. I hate it. I hate saying this to you. I wish I could say fuck the Army but I can't! You've got to take responsibility for what you've done.'

'I know, I know, I know!'

He walked up and down more rapidly now.

'You'll have to serve some time for this, so fucking what!'

'I can't make that call!'

'Face reality.'

'I hate reality.'

'We all hate reality when it hurts but there's nothing else. God knows, I've tried to find fairyland but it doesn't exist. There's only reality and you have to give of your best.'

Jonny walked rapidly up and down the room. It was only a small room so he was constantly turning, making Joy's head swim and stomach churn.

'That's all there is, you can't have a buzz a minute. You've got to start growing up, you've got to overcome those hopeless feelings. Accept things, and you begin to find peace, then perhaps your dreams will come, in the end.'

'I've got no dreams. The Sergeant-Major shouted at me!'

'So what, other people get shouted at.'

'No, Mum, they don't, not what he shouted at me. He shouted and he screamed and he didn't show me no respect.'

'You have to earn respect. You should have tried to do what he told you.'

'I did try.'

'You should have tried harder.'

'I tried as hard as I could.'

'Then he should have showed you respect.'

And Joy knew that she too had run from Big Tom when he screamed and shouted at her. She too hadn't been able to bear the sneering and the bullying.

She'd read in the paper about people being beaten up in the Army. About soldiers hanging themselves through bullying, and she thought: Supposing that happens to my Jonny, and her heart stopped in horror. In the shock and pity of it all, she turned away.

Then turning back she caught his hand.

'Jonny, Jonny, you should have stayed with Jackie.'

'She didn't want me, Mum,' said Jonny.

And Joy let go of his hand.

'Why do you think it's so important to stay alive, Mum? Perhaps it doesn't matter. Perhaps it's as good being dead as alive. Think like that, then you'll be free of worrying about me.'

'Don't talk of it, Jonny. You know I'd lie down and never get up if something happened to you.'

And she looked at him, she looked into his eyes till he turned away.

'Come on, let's go and do your bed, Gladys.'

And going into Gladys's flat, Joy is unhinged by misery – he'll get nicked sooner or later, it hurts, it really hurts – and dilapidation. Gladys's dilapidation. The carriage clock lay on its side ('It loses time if I stand it upright so I keep it on its side') so Joy had to bend her head sideways to see the time.

'I'm fed up, Mum.'

'You're fed up, what about me?'

Gladys coughed and coughed again and drew on her fag. The ash was nearly falling off the end as the two of them changed the sheets and pillow cases. Joy shook out the pink eiderdown.

'Look at all the burns in this. One day you'll really catch yourself alight and that will be that.'

'I've got to have a fag in the night. You don't expect me just to lie there, do you?'

'And you've blackened all the ceiling above your grill again. You should read the notice.'

Joy had put a big notice over the cooker. MUM, WATCH THE GRILL, TURN IT OFF!

'This is my house, I'm doing what I like in it.'

'Yes, but it's me that's got to wash all the ceiling down.'

'The council will have to do it.'

'They won't do it, they did your whole kitchen a couple of years ago.'

'Oh never mind.'

Joy bundled all the dirty clothes into an orange plastic bag and put them ready to take next door to wash.

'Here, Joy, I remember now. I was in the Regal when the pains started with you. I can't remember the film now. I used to know it. Oh yes, it's come to me, *Gone with the Wind*, that was it, *Gone with the Wind*, Clark Gable, I liked him. I was getting the pains all around my back, night-time came and my waters broke. "Send for the nurse!" I hollered. Bill had to run round to her house.'

'We'll hang your new paper next weekend,' said Joy.

The flat badly needed decorating. The hall with its brown-and-silver-leaf pattern. She'd done that herself about twenty years ago. She hated the sight of it now. The curved cocktail bar they'd clubbed up for and given Gladys for her fiftieth birthday, it was all the rage then with its red-glass sliding doors and bar stools to match in cream-and-red laminated wood and glass panels that lit up when you switched it on. It even had red glasses to match.

'Dust the bar, Gladys, it's filthy.'

'That bar has seen plenty of life, Joy.'

And Glad's face lit up. It had definitely seen some drinking. Had it just. Then she felt a spasm of pain shoot through her leg wiping the smile off her face.

'My leg hurts.'

'It's your age.'

'It didn't used to hurt.'

'I said it's your age.'

'I'm not that old.'

'No, but you are eighty.'

'Eighty's not that old.'

'It's old enough to have a leg that hurts.'

Gladys looked in the mirror.

'I don't look bad for eighty, do I?'

But Joy didn't answer. A bad fairy had come down and left a grey film over her eyes and a creepy-crawly web all over her body covering her from top to toe in a faintly sticky mucus, tasteless and scentless, invisible yet absolute.

Everything around her was drab and, more than drab, downright ugly. She saw the burns on the green velour settee, covered with a rug. The rug had slipped. She saw the chipped mugs given away by the garage. She saw the brown-and-green-flowered carpet with the bare patch where Gladys walked up and down, the worn path between the kitchen and the settee. She saw the cheap ornaments she'd brought her back from her escapades to Spain. She saw the brown sitting-room curtains bought from a boot sale last year. She saw the yellowing nets with the crinoline ladies in rows.

Sometimes everything goes wrong and I don't seem to be able to make it go right.

'You've dropped your fag-ends in the sink again and I'm not cleaning them up.'

'You're too fussy.'

And when everything was clean and tidy Joy went back into her own house.

The music was going strong in the front room. Jonny had only been out twice since Jeff left and then only over the road to buy cigarettes. A couple of times he'd slipped out of the house at night taking Joy's keys.

He was driving her nuts. She knew it would only be a matter of time before the authorities tracked him down. In the meantime she wasn't going to turn him out on to the street. She couldn't do that. He was her son. Stomp, stomp. Gladys was in again.

'You going out, Joy?'

'Yes, I told you. I'm going over Carol's. You're going down to Teddy for your dinner.'

'I'm not going down there. I'm coming with you.'

She thought of the cruise with George, how ill she'd been and how George was a good fairy.

'George was a good fairy on that cruise, Joy,' she said.

Now he was dead. If he hadn't died she could be out and about with him now. He always bought her presents, had something in his pocket, every time she saw him: a little bottle of perfume, a real silk scarf, things a woman likes to get from a man. Teddy never bought her nothing.

Gladys went out on to the walkway and poked at her window boxes. A slug-coloured sky hung over the flats, damp on her cheeks, mizzling damp all around.

'You can't see 'em there, those antirrhinums we put in,' she said.

'No, because they haven't come up. These are all dead, I'll take them out.'

Joy used her serving spoon as a trowel to dig in the thin earth.

'Leave the yellow ones, they aren't finished yet.'

'Fucking hell, aren't they strong.'

'I said, leave 'em.'

'Oh do them yourself then. I'm not helping you.'

And Joy went back indoors. A cold wind blew across the balcony catching the back of Gladys's skirt and whisking it up around her knees as she jabbed at the earth. The yellow plastic windmill spun in the breeze. Her hair blew back and she screwed up her eyes.

Jonny came out of the front room leaving the music turned up and asked for a couple of quid and Joy slammed them down on the kitchen table. Her courage had run out like sand through the glass, her heart was a black stone that had slid into her stomach and Jonny, shoulders hunched in his thin white T-shirt, crept out and across the road to the off-licence for a packet of fags.

For a moment the wind dropped, the sun came out and a bird sang in the lime trees. Joy opened her door on to the walkway and went out. But it really was cold, thought Joy, as she swept the balcony in her coat and bedroom slippers clear of leaves and earth dropped by Gladys from her window-box activities. She'd be over to Carol's in a minute. Carol was doing roast beef and Yorkshire for dinner. She'd left something in the fridge for Jonny.

Suddenly she heard shouting and a yowl and another and another, an animal howl, a desperate scream of fear, and she knew it was Jonny, and even before she knew she knew she was already halfway down the concrete stairs and out into the road and she saw the Military Police car and two of them with Jonny up against the wall, his fist in the air. And as she flew across the road towards him he was grabbed and fell, grappling and yelling, to the pavement.

'Stand back!' someone shouted at Joy as she hurtled towards him and the second policeman caught her arm, halting her flight, and she too fell.

'Stay away, lady.'

'That's my son.'

'Leave him alone.'

'He's my son.'

'Go away, Mum.'

He was quiet now as they led him towards the car.

'He's got no coat,' said Joy.

'Give me yours,' said Jonny.

She took off her coat and handed it to him. They released his arms and he put it on and got in the van.

'I'm all right now,' he said. 'Go indoors.'

And when she stood there, 'Go away, Mum. I'm no good.'

Teddy went into hospital. Joy took Gladys up to see him and on the way home Glad said, 'Here, now we're all on our own, got no husbands or blokes, we could go away and have a good time. I could soon find someone.'

THE CARAVAN

Carol's sister had a caravan at Selsey Bill and when Carol told her all about Jonny she said, 'Joy and Glad can have the caravan for the weekend. It won't cost them nothing.' So here they were in the car heading south.

They drove deeper and deeper into the country. Joy took the back lanes now which the little Fiat liked. The banks and hedges were bright with pink campion and buttercups. Gladys sneezed.

'God Bless.'

'Hay fever.'

'It'll go once you get to the sea. Look at the apple blossom.'

They stopped at a pub for Guinness and sandwiches. They sat in the garden. The house martins swooped in and out from under the thatch. Little feathers glistened in the light. In and out. In and out. Now a finch joined them, bustling about among the twigs, shaking the clematis flowers and singing.

On they went past Goodwood Racecourse. Joy had opened the roof and let in the sun. She smelt the air. It was mild and sweet. She already felt better.

'I had some terrific days with George at Goodwood, Joy. Remember when he had that big win on Empire Gold and he took me on that cruise? When we handed in the passports they found out we wasn't married. "You can't share a cabin if you're not married." "We've been living together for years," I said. "Well, you can't do it here." '

There were dog roses out in the hedgerow. They caught at the car when Joy stopped and pulled in close to let another driver pass. She fancied she could smell the sea already. She longed for the sea.

Gladys went on talking and Joy let it wash over her.

'No one would speak to us after that. Everyone knew we wasn't married. One dirty old sod put his arms round me. George thought there was something in it from the way he was looking at me. Wanted to pick a fight with him.'

They turned off down a lane past a farm shop. Cows were standing under a tree chewing the cud and swishing their tails.

'. . . he splashed all his winnings on that cruise. Then they wouldn't let us share a cabin. They put him on the top deck and me down below. I got seasick. He was like a little fairy. Up and down, up and down. Trying to look after me. Yes, he was a good fairy to me when I was seasick. I never told you about that, did I, Joy?'

'Only a hundred times, Mum.'

'George liked a bit of sport, same as I do. Did you lock my door?'

'Yes, both locks.'

'Did you pack the sheets?'

'Yes, in your bag. You didn't take them out, did you?'

'The bag was too full.'

'Oh Gladys, now we've only one pair of sheets between us.'

'Don't be wild, Joy.'

'I am wild.'

'We were only talking about them last night.'

'That was the last thing I said, "The sheets are in your bag." '

'I was up half the night walking up and down.'

'Well, we'll both have to sleep in the settee-bed tonight. If we can open it.'

'I'm not sleeping without sheets.'

'No, I said, you're sleeping in with me. Look, Mum, over there, the sea!'

And Joy's heart leapt and for a full thirty seconds she forgot it was broken. She forgot about Jeff and Jonny, so exciting it was, to catch a glimpse of the sea.

'You always slept in with me from when you were born. Bill slept in his own room. I only slept with him now and again. I always had you in bed with me.'

'I slept with you right up until I got married. Even after I got married and I had a row with Tom I always come home and got into bed with you.'

'I used to send my sheets every week to the Sunshine Laundry. I was ever so particular.'

'I remember going there with you. You had a pair with roses on, they were lovely.'

'I got them off the tally man. I had all the sheets off of him. Red roses and yellow roses. I always had a lovely bed.'

'How many pairs of net curtains you got, Mum?'

'Long ones or short? I keep buying net curtains. I love a bit of net, I don't know why. I've got a friend down here but I don't know if she's alive or dead.'

'Enid, she sent you a Christmas card.'

'That was a long time ago. I hope Teddy isn't going up my flat.'

'He's in hospital.'

'Well, I hope he doesn't come out early and take that ginger bird up there.'

'She wouldn't have him.'

'He ain't no use anyway. We've never had connections. He couldn't do it. I tried. In fact I fell off the bleeding bed through it but it was no good.' Gladys straightened her scarf and looked in the mirror. 'I know he's got somebody else.'

'No he hasn't, Mum.'

'I saw him talking to that ginger bird. Let him go. I'll get someone else.' She looked again in the mirror. 'I'm not bad for eighty. They think I'm only seventy. I'd love a young man if I could get hold of one. If you find a good one hang on to him. I don't know why you ever let Jeff go. Look, Joy, the sea!'

'I saw it five minutes ago.'

'Well, why didn't you tell me?'

* * *

At last they turned in at the gateway of the Blue Bird Caravan Park and bumped along the tarmac track over the humps past a myriad of caravans.

'Give me that piece of paper, Mum. Turn left at Mudlark.'

'Oh, it has changed.'

'It's not surprising. We haven't been here for twenty years.'

'It's all changed. Last time I was here I was working at the baths. Dad's been dead twenty-five years. If he were to wake up and see us now he'd be in his glory.'

'There's Mudlark.' Joy read out the directions. ' "Turn left. Take the second-left and Warrior Queen is the third on the right." '

'Not many people about.'

'It's early in the season. There it is, Warrior Queen.'

'Pull up then.'

'Give me a chance.'

But Gladys had already opened her door and was struggling out.

'I'll take the handbags, you take the cases.'

They unlocked the door and went inside.

Glad looked around. Inside it was all pale pink and mushroom. Even the bath and toilet were pink.

'It was port-wine red and the bedroom was Wedgwood-blue with cupids over the bed. What have they done?'

'This is a brand-new caravan. Come and look at this toilet, Mum.'

'We didn't have a toilet. We went over there to the brick building. Remember? There were hot-water showers and all, over there. It was spotless.'

'In the night it was a bucket,' said Joy.

'We might see Duchess if we take a walk over there.'

'No, she's dead.'

'They're all dead?'

'Monarch is gone. June's gone. Maureen is gone. Her son Robert died from leukaemia.'

'We had some fun. Caravans were all the rage then. Remember when we danced, Joy? That night when the caravan rocked from side to side.'

'I thought it was going to tip and we all had to run to the other end.'

'Maureen went out with Jack Sullivan. Have they got married yet?'

'Married? They were married twenty years ago. He's dead now.'

'What about Jean? Her husband went off with someone else, didn't he?'

'Jean went into hospital to have her veins done. The next day she was dead.'

'Jeanie dead! She could drink and fight. Couldn't she fight when she'd had a drink. I can't believe she's dead. She was too lively.'

'It was Mother's Day the day she died.'

'I wonder what became of Tom Doyle?'

'He's dead.'

'You don't know what become of him.'

'Well, if he's still alive he's ninety-odd.'

'He can't be more than sixty.'

'He was sixty thirty years ago, Mum.'

'He must be dead then. Bill was on late shift so I took Tom Doyle down to the caravan.'

'I came the next day with Jonny and you'd had a row.'

'Jonny loved the caravan, didn't he, Joy? Happy as the day was long down here. Always timid, wasn't he? Didn't want to play with the other kids.'

'Always wanted to be with us.'

'I don't know why he ever joined the Army.'

'No, you could have fooled me. Remember when he started at the comprehensive I gave that big kid a pound a week to watch out over Jonny in case he got beaten up? A pound a week, that cost me, the whole of his first year. Then Jonny heard about it and he was wild.'

'Funny kid, he's never been right since he fell out of that tree.'

'Come out on this deck. You can see the sea.'

They stood side by side on the wooden deck and there, over a tangled hedge strung about with columbines and across a shingly beach, stretched a dark-grey sea.

'Isn't it beautiful? I can smell it,' said Joy.

'You can't smell the sea.'

'I can.'

'It's nice here. You couldn't ask for nothing better. Nobody interferes with you. You can get up and go out and do what you like. I'd buy one if I had the money.'

Then they went to the pub and had a drink.

'Haven't I seen her somewhere before? I'm sure I used to go out with her husband. He had a big spotted dog. Now her husband's dead and so is the dog. You won't ever put me away, will you?'

'No, I won't put you away but I don't want to give up my whole life to you.'

'What?'

'I said, I don't want to put my whole life around you.'

'I don't want you to. People think that because we live next door to one another we're always in each other's houses but we're not.'

'We are most of the time, Mum.'

'I'm mostly in your house, you're not in mine. When your mother goes you won't have nobody to fill her place.'

'No, of course I won't. Whatever made you say that?'

'I think about it.'

'Well, don't, because I won't ever put you in a home, Mum.'

'I haven't had what I really wanted out of my life, Joy. I always imagined myself living down the country and having visitors. I'd like to have married a man who had something. If I'd have married a nice comfortable man I'd have been a very happy woman. I've had a lot of strain. I've tried and tried and tried but it wasn't to be.'

'But we was happy, Mum, when I was a kid. We was happy.'

'Yes, when I come to think of it, I haven't had a bad life. Every Sunday we'd have rock cakes for tea.'

'I used to lick the bowl.'

Joy went to get another drink and Gladys sat thinking . . .

I'd do all my ironing Sunday afternoon. All the clothes would be hanging round on hangers. I loved doing my ironing. It was nice. I was happy.

It was an awful shock when Bill died. I was talking to him five minutes before he died . . . 'You look after her and she'll look after you,' he said. I thought he'd be out of hospital in a couple of days . . . 'See you tomorrow,' I said, when I left, and when I got home the phone rang and it was the hospital to say he'd died. I couldn't make it out.

All they gave me when he died was a thousand pounds for the funeral and five hundred pounds for myself. Where it went I don't know. They never give me a pension like they did everybody else. Some wives get pensions for the rest of their lives but I never.

'Mind you, I made it last. I went about four years before I was broke.'

'What?' said Joy coming back with the drinks.

'Dad's pension. I made it last.'

And Gladys was off again and Joy thought of her father. She always thought about him when she was down, about how she had been the apple of his eye, and that comforted her.

'Let's go and find some fish and chips, Mum.'

They ate fish and chips and then in the dark made their way back.

'Lucky there's a moon. We'd never find it.'

The columbines shone bright white in the black hedge.

'Look at the sky.'

'All those stars.'

Joy pulled out the fold-away bed and put on the sheets.

'If you hadn't forgotten those sheets we could have each had a bed to ourselves, Mum.'

'Never mind.'

'I've always loved your laundered sheets. Carol slept under coats whereas we had laundered sheets.'

'Granny used to say to me, "Always keep your bed clean, Gladys." And I always have.'

'And a big bolster in a bolster case.'

'What?'

'I was just remembering the bolster on your bed.'

'Oh.'

Gladys put on her two hairnets before she got undressed. One pink, one blue. Then she took off her clothes and folded them neatly and put on her nightdress and her dressing gown.

'This used to be yours.'

'No, I got it in a boot sale.'

'I hope you washed it.'

'It's been washed a hundred times.'

Gladys got in first, up against the wall, and then Joy eased in beside her.

'Where's the bucket, Joy, in case I need it?'

'There's a toilet. You've just used it.'

'Oh I forgot.'

'Good-night, Mum.'

'Good-night, love.'

They both slept.

Later Gladys woke. She turned this way and that and woke Joy.

'That fish is rising on me.'

'You ate too fast.'

'That fish has risen.'

'Go back to sleep,' said Joy.

'What time is it?'

'It's three o'clock in the morning.'

'Are the doors locked?'

'Yes.'

Joy couldn't get back to sleep. She thought of Jonny . . .

Carol says I spoilt him when Tom was away in prison but I thought by giving him everything I was doing the right thing. Perhaps I should have pushed him more at school. I did tell him I wanted to see him get on. 'I'd like to see you do something worthwhile with your life, Jonny,' I said.

Now he was locked up and she was racked with fear. Why hadn't she protected him from the dangerous world?

And when she could no longer bear to think about Jonny she thought about Jeff. She remembered the weekend they'd gone to Amsterdam on the forty thousand petrol stamps they'd saved between them.

She is riding on a tram in Amsterdam. Jeff is beside her and suddenly through the window of the tram, they are sitting upstairs, she sees down into a shop window, plate glass shining, a pair of bright-green sandals. 'I want those, Jeff,' and she runs down the stairs, nearly tripping. 'Wait, Joy, till it stops.' 'We won't find the shop,' and she flies through the air towards the pavement, Jeff after her, nearly landing on top of her. They make their way to the shoe shop and buy the green sandals.

Next door was a sex shop and Jeff bought her a gold mask and a gold dog collar with long spikes and gold anklets. And they went back to their hotel room and she took off all her clothes and put on her green sandals and Jeff helped her buckle on the gold dog collar and fasten her gold anklets. And she went to close the curtains and looked down out of the window at the dark canal and the tall houses opposite. Then she shut the curtains so only a glimmer of afternoon sun entered. Enough to catch the gold in her dog collar and to make her anklets and green sandals shine.

Joy felt tears well and ebb, a few squeezed out on to her cheeks. Her head ached and she tried to calm herself and sleep but she was invaded by a past she couldn't let go of and as soon as Jeff vanished from sight Gladys loomed up luminous and vast filling her horizon, crowding each corner of her mind.

Her and my dad. She's wearing a big kiss-me-Kate hat and a white dress with great big black polka dots on it.

She's in Bobby's Club waltzing with Arthur and singing along . . . 'Spanish eyes . . . those Spanish eyes loll, la-la-la-la . . . the look in your eyes and mine . . . wait for me . . .'

She's looking after the cars outside Chelsea Football Ground wearing a coffee-coloured coat with a big collar and a turban. She's directing a car backwards. Her hand is in the air. 'Come on, this way . . . whoa . . .'

Now she's in her black suit, white blouse, white clip-on earrings and a white necklace. Her red toe-nails are peeping out of white sling-backs. I can see her at an outing laughing. She's chatting everyone up. Her eyes are firing all over the place.

Now I see her with her hair blue-tinted wearing a lemon dress with a pink-and-blue tie-up at the neck in pink and pale-blue spots. She liked that dress, went back and bought the same one in lime. She was with George then and she was working in the kiosk in

Earls Court Station. She always had a shopping bag with her.

Joy turned over and tried to sleep but the pictures kept on coming.

We're at the Bridge House in Reigate. My dad has just died. She has had his insurance money and she took us to a hotel. Her hair is blue and she's got a net over it with little pearls on it. Some of her hair is caught in the pearls. She's got a black dress on with black-net sleeves. It's Christmas and she's got a gin and tonic in her hand and she's laughing.

Now I see her in her old dress doing her window boxes and looking out for me over the balcony.

We're going out. She puts on her Max Factor crème puff candleglow and her red lipstick on her cupid-bow lips. 'Does that look all right?' 'No, I've got to do your eyebrows.' I shave her eyebrows into shape. She looks in the mirror. 'I don't look eighty now.'

Joy felt there was no room for her anywhere. She lay still and hoped that Gladys had fallen asleep but she hadn't.

'It was that batter on the fish made it rise. You awake, Joy?'

'No, Mum.'

'I must have a fag. I wonder what Teddy's up to? That ginger woman will probably be visiting him up the hospital and promising to feed the cat.'

'No, his neighbour is going to feed the cat. You just think like that because you were always two-timing Dad.'

'He's had another woman, don't you worry yourself.'

Gladys got up to go to the toilet. Joy got herself a fag

and opened the door on to the deck and looked out. The moon shivered on the sea.

'Come and look at the stars, Mum.'

'I've got that pain in my chest.'

'See how the water glistens.'

Gladys joined her at the open door.

'It's shining. Your father used to use marge paper to wipe over his hair to make it shine. Then he'd put a little curl in it with his finger.

'I'll never forget when you was born. I lay in that bed and he lifted you up in the air and he said, "You're my little girl, you're my glory." I said, "I've got her now and I'll never let her go." At least we've stuck to one another, Joy,' said Gladys.

'Fucking hell, have we!'

'I like the sea. The night I met George I pinned him up against the wall. The moon was full that night and all. "I've never had a woman like you in my life." "How many women have you had then?" I said. "Only my wife and she didn't like it." So I taught him different ways. "That's filth," he said, "I don't want anything to do with you." "You will," I said. Well, after that he went out and bought me a pure camel coat and took me on a cruise.'

'Let's go back to bed, Glad.'

'I hope he didn't tell anyone the things I showed him.'

Joy shut the door and they climbed in together.

'Move over.'

'I think a love of the sea might run in the family. Granny had a friend who was captain of a ship. He used to come up the river to the marble factory. She met him in the Crabtree and he'd buy her a drink of an afternoon and she'd wash all his shirts.'

'You're always on about fellows.'

'Some women like carrying on and some women don't believe in it. I like carrying on and seeing a bit of life.'

'Go to sleep, Mum.'

'That fish is rising again.'

'Shut up about that fish. It's probably swimming about in there having a great time.'

'It's going to jump right up my throat in a minute.'

'It's three o'clock in the morning.'

'Night-night, Joy.'

'Night, Mum.'

Early morning, the sun slid across the grass. Green beneath the shadow of the thorn tree, deep and still. Little puddles gleamed between the roots. And all the reeds in the boggy corner were covered in spiders' webs, glistening in the light.

They were both awake. Joy opened the door of the caravan. Outside it was wet and green. Some tiny seapinks clustered in pin cushions on the wall, clusters of whitish pinkish flowers and little birds singing and flitting about. Dragon-flies hovered over the ditch.

She watched the swallows shooting over the stagnant ditch. Darting dangerously near the shining green water and up and off again. Are they playing? No, that one caught a fly.

'Mum, I saw a swallow catch a fly.'

'What?'

Gladys stood in the doorway of the caravan in a sleeveless flowered nightdress combing her hair.

'What's for breakfast, Joy?'

'I heard a cuckoo and listen, another one singing back. It's lucky, isn't it, when two cuckoos sing to each other?'

'I can't hear nothing.'

'That's because you're deaf. Listen.'

They sang on. It started to rain.

'It rained that time I came down here with Tom Doyle. After I'd been with him I found lice in my hat and I burnt it. It was a nice little hat but I wouldn't wear it no more. I threw it on the fire.'

Gladys sat on the toilet with the door open, her thin leg sticking out sideways, talking the while.

'I was going to marry him but it was too late. He got cancer and died in the same ward as my Bill. They all died on me. Someone said, "You killed them with kindness." I don't know where the kindness come in.'

Joy cooked the breakfast. Bacon, eggs, sausages, tomatoes. Outside it began to rain hard. Gladys combed her hair.

'Is Irene in her caravan?'

'Irene's dead.'

Glad stood at the sink and washed under her nightgown. She soaped her flannel, and wiped under her arms, and then lifting up first one foot, and then the other, she soaped each of them, like two delicate birds that might fly away. She rinsed out the flannel and wiped them clean.

'What shall I put on? My red dress?'

'No, don't put your best dress on. It's too cold.'

'Where are we going today, Joy?'

'Nowhere.'

'Nowhere!' Gladys looked out of the window. Nobody about. 'It's dead. Open the window. I'm too hot.'

'Shall I turn the fire off?'

'Yes, turn the fire off.'

It rained all morning and it was muddy outside.

'We'd best go home. There's nothing here. I've got an upset stomach,' said Glad.

'You eat too much.'

'It was the fish.'

The rain and wind flew in rapid gusts at the windows. All the petals from the dog roses were scattered on the grass.

'I put those chairs out last night thinking it would be nice today,' said Joy.

Two moorhens ran in a puddle and disappeared under the caravan next door.

'Don't drop your ash on the carpet.'

'It's cold in here. Haven't they got no heating?'

'You were too hot a moment ago.'

'Where did you put my knickers?'

'Where did you put them?'

'I packed three pairs. Where are they now?'

The hedgerow trees were blown into flat topknots by the sea wind. The rain glanced off the may blossom, hit the window and cascaded down the glass.

'Shall we have a nice cup of tea?'

'No, let's go out and find the site where the old caravan used to be,' said Joy.

'It'll have changed so much we'll never recognise it.'

'We will.'

Joy drove across the wet grass and stopped under a tree.

'I'm going to get out. You stay there.'

She went to the edge of the stream and called over her shoulder.

'They've cleaned this up. It used to be a sea of mud.'

Gladys opened the door.

'Stop there. It's raining.'

Joy wanted to be alone for a moment. She stood under a tree and watched a family of moorhens dabble in and out of the rushes.

Jonny loved the moorhens. He'd bring his breakfast out and sit under this tree and throw them tiny bits of bread. He reckoned he could tame them but he never did. She and Big Tom and Jonny had come down nearly every weekend to the old caravan. They'd had a bit of proper family life before Tom went to prison. They'd been happy enough. He wasn't the same person when he came out. And now Jonny. She'd known he'd get nicked for this sooner or later, but it did hurt. Fucking hell, did it. And she heard his voice, 'I'm no good, Mum.'

My poor Jonny, I wish I could make it all come right and I know I can't.

Gladys had got out of the car and was coming over.

'It's brightening up.'

'I told you it would.'

Miraculously the rain stopped. The sun came out and shone on the clean bright grass and the gleaming side of the plastic caravan. A butterfly settled on a gorse bush bright with flower.

'Remember our first one, blue-and-white aluminium with the steps in the middle?'

It had a coal fire that heated the water and a big bed right across the end.

'You paid a hundred pounds for that from Tom Doyle. All through me, that was. He fancied me, thought he was on to something,' said Gladys.

'It was a bargain.'

'Men knew how to spend in those days. Not like now, you go into a pub and no one offers you fuck all.'

'Well, you are eighty, Mum.'

'What's that got to do with it?'

'Let's go across the little bridge and find somewhere to sit in the sun.'

'That's the wood over there where Jonny saw the snake.'

'We'll be all right. Hang on to me.'

Going into the wood. It was dark at first.

'Come back out into the sun. I don't want to go in there, Joy. There might be snakes.'

Tiny wood anemones grew along the bank and everywhere may trees thick with blossom and young hazelnuts with the light shining through their pale-green leaves.

And then they came upon the bluebells.

'Look, Mum, the bluebells.'

Startling in their vividness. Such a giddy blue and gaudy. Yet so beautiful. So many of them.

'Let's pick some for the caravan.'

Two heads bent and silent picking. Chaffinches singing.

'This is making me dizzy.'

'Sit down on that tree then.'

And Glad sat on a fallen trunk and Joy went on picking, greedy in her desire for the flowers. Gladys watched her.

'Come on, that's enough.'

'We're not in a hurry.'

'I'm hungry.'

'You're always hungry.'

She watched Joy straighten up and saw her face, as she cradled her enormous bunch of bluebells in her arms, reflect the light blueish white in the dark wood, and then speckled by sun through leaves, and suddenly all lit up as she reached the little clearing among the young beech trees where Gladys sat, saw her blonde hair all bright in the sunshine. And she remembered when Joy ran away to Australia with John.

I nearly went mad when she went to Australia. I was on the piss all the time. I was with Arthur then. I used to cry and he used to say, 'It's no good crying, my girl, that won't fetch her back.'

'I was on that fucking phone every night when you was in Australia. I had a phone bill of a hundred and odd pounds.'

'Six hundred, Mum. They cut the phone off. I had to get you one in another name.'

'I used to say to Arthur, "I wonder what she's doing. I wonder if she's all right." He got fed up. "I've never seen a woman like you. Worry like that. She's gone. Let her get on with it." I pinched his money to try and save enough to go out there. I made my mind up to go out there. In the end he said, "I'll give you some money. Go out to your daughter. You drive me mad." Then you said you was coming home, so I didn't go.'

That morning Joy came home I was there to meet her. I didn't know where Southampton was. I had to find it all out. She got in at six o'clock in the morning.

'When I got there they said the boat was in dock but they couldn't let people off for a while.'

I'm waiting there and she comes flying down the gang plank with her blonde hair and her fucking case and she didn't care a sod. She had this bleeding cape round her.

'I can see you now waving your hand.'

'I had on a white suit because I was golden brown.'

'You were white blonde. Gleaming blonde.'

'It was the sun in Australia.'

'We went on the piss that night and the next day. We went up the club.'

'The next night I ended up in hospital.'

'How did you end up in hospital, Joy?'

'Big Tom done me, didn't he?'

'Oh yes, Big Tom done you.'

'I was petrified.'

'I ran away. He was drunk. I thought he was going to hit me and all. Anyway, old Arthur was good, you come to us.'

'I looked like a bull dog. My eyes were like a boxer's.'

'He was like Telly Savalas, Arthur was, lovely bald head.'

'He didn't have a bald head, Mum. He had lovely white hair.'

'He had a bald head. I should know.'

They walked back to the car. Joy carried the bluebells. The smell was wonderful. 'Can you catch the scent?'

'They don't smell.'

'Yes they do.'

'Well, I can't smell nothing. I think I lost it when I had that bad abortion. I nearly died. The Old Man was happy when he saw me pregnant because he knew nobody else would have me.

'I used to lend Granny his things to pawn and he'd look in the chest of drawers to see if they was there. "Fuck him," she'd say, "I need the money." "Hurry up and get them back," I'd say. So she'd take in some washing to get his trousers out of pawn. "Don't touch my things!" he'd say and Granny would come round for them and I'd say, "No, Mum, you can't have them no more." "Lend me them," she'd say, "I'll get them back for you." In the end he said, "Your mother's a fucking nuisance keep coming round here borrowing my clothes for her beer." And that was the finish of it.

'Funny, Granny always came to me. You'd have thought she'd have gone to Aggie, she was the oldest. She married a widower. He was a terrible sod, he was. Then there was Ethel. Ethel never went outside the door, not here. Then there was Ben, he went out to Canada. Then there was Emmy. Then come Alice. Then come Rose. Then me.

'Hang on a minute, let me start again. Ben, Aggie, Ethel, Sid, Ginny. She died in an old people's home. She was ninety-four. Sid . . . I don't know what became of Sid. He died, I expect. Emmy, she died. Ginny . . . Rose, she died. Jack, he died of pneumonia. Alice died young. She went to America and died. She sent me a fox fur from New York.'

'Hold up, Mum, the bridge is slippery.'

In the afternoon they put the deck-chairs out. There were people about now the sun was out.

'Here, look at that sun. I can feel it warming my skin,' said Gladys.

'Move over, you're keeping it off me.'

A thrush sang in fits and starts. Two pale-blue butterflies hovered over the hedge. And Joy longed for Jeff, and a glut of tears rose up and spat out of her eyes on to her cheeks.

Gladys sat watching the kids playing and the grown-ups pottering. Women sitting in the sun. Someone called out, 'Hi, nice afternoon.' And Gladys told her all about the caravan they had years ago and Joy in a deck-chair beside her fell asleep listening to it, her head on one side.

'I hope she doesn't burn,' said Gladys, and she draped a towel over the awning to protect Joy from the sun.

And come the evening they cooked a chicken in the caravan and Joy made the table pretty with pink-paper napkins stuck in the glasses and the bluebells in a big jug. And after they had eaten the delicious chicken and drunk the lager they sat out on the deck and smoked a few fags and drank some more lager and looked at the speckled grey sea and the long shingly headland and saw two cormorants and loads of seagulls and a black dog running in and out of the water in the last of the light.

However beautiful Joy made her flat inside, and it was beautiful and spotless and polished, she always had to face the estate out of the window. The endless identical blocks of concrete flats standing on acres of grass, muddy in winter, bone dry and yellow in summer, and strewn with this and that and whoever you met at the shops or on the ramp it was people with huge problems and she was sick of problems, sick of crying over Jonny. Sick to death of the drabness of it all. She understood why Jeff had left, he wanted something better and in her heart she didn't blame him. She wished she could stay here for ever by the sea.

At last the sun set and they went inside and got undressed and went to bed.

And in the night Joy had a dream.

Humphrey Bogart had this shop and in the window was an opulent silver-and-mother-of-pearl cabinet and I said, 'I want that.' And Jeff said, 'You can't have it,' and I said, 'I want it, I want it, and that's all there is to it.' And I asked how much it was and it was very expensive and I said, 'I don't think I've got enough money but I want it.'

I opened it up and inside I saw this beautiful pair of silver shoes, high-heeled shoes, and I put them on and they fitted me like gloves and I said, 'These shoes were made for me.' And I kept looking at my feet and I felt wonderful and Jeff said, 'Where are you going to put this cabinet? You haven't got the room.' And I said, 'I'll chuck everything out, I'm going to have it.'

And I turned back to explore the little drawers and cubby-holes. The first one I opened smelt like soot in an abandoned coal cellar. It was full of such a dark dark, darker than black velvet, I drew back in fright. Bogart offered me a cigarette and I took one and put it to my lips. He leant towards me and lit it. 'Open your eyes wide and LOOK, only look, and you will penetrate the darkness. When it is too dark to see your shoes, you will feel them, softly holding your feet.' I peered into the dark and saw shot-silk black with shadows.

And in the shot-silk there were seams of light and pinpoints of brightness that reflected back behind the darkness hidden pictures, and Joy's curiosity was aroused by reflections beyond reflections, by the dancing lights of fires at night and a bare-chested man washing by a standpipe at a fairground. What she saw quickly faded into more darkness. Inky dark shadows without light or hope. And then again on the brink of despair she saw light. A spider's web had grown across the entrance of one of the cubby-holes and as she peered through the threads she saw an open view across countryside she'd never visited.

In some of the darkest nooks the blackness was deeper than the deepest shade but her eyes had grown accustomed to the dark and she'd learn to find her way. She knew Bogey was watching her. She felt the ground solid beneath the soles of her silver shoes. 'Only remember, one foot in front of the other,' he said, and her heart quickened, she heard it beat.

And when she woke she crept outside leaving Gladys asleep.

Never had the night seemed so soft. She was enchanted by the night itself. Was it because the moon was suspended in a bright mist and a single sliver of light rippled on the sea? The trees were her mysterious friends looming out of the dark. The grass beneath her bare feet was wet and caressing. The silence stretched out into eternity enticing her on. No, wait. That thrilling song. Was it a nightingale? She had never heard a nightingale but Jeff had heard one once and told her, 'When you hear it, you know it's a nightingale.' Joy knew it was a nightingale. She felt the breeze through her thin nightdress on her naked body and with this sense of nakedness came acute pleasure. And nothing really mattered. She was alive and that was enough. She felt full of hope. And in some fresh intangible way she knew once again where she was going.

Next day they packed up and drove home. They had a good run. The little car flew along. Gladys dozed and looked out of the window, good as gold, and Joy thought about Jonny and now she knew his adventure was his own. His struggles were his struggles and hers were hers. She knew whatever he was going to have to go through, however many dragons were going to jump out at him, his life belonged to him and she need no longer watch over him. Instead she would send him love each morning when she woke and, each night before she went to sleep, she would send him sweet dreams.

I've made a hell of a lot of mistakes but I'm not a failure. I know I'm not because I don't feel a failure. I'm going to learn Spanish and I'm going to talk Spanish by the end of the year. I feel cocky with myself. Mum can think what she likes, I'm going to learn Spanish. I'm so pleased with myself and I haven't even begun yet. And next time I meet someone I'm going to say, 'Before you start, I've got a mother with senile dementia, early stages, my son is a deserter from the Army and I live in a council flat, and if you want me for who I am then you can have me with open arms.'

They walked up the concrete ramp. Joy in front carrying the cases. Glad close behind with the handbags. Jeff was standing at the entrance.

'What are you doing here, Jeff?'

'I can't live without you, Joy.'

'Get rid of him,' said Gladys, 'he ain't no good.'

But Joy only heard her as background music out of the corner of her ear. She put down the suitcases. Jeff picked them up. She took her bag and found her keys. She unlocked the door. Her hand was trembling. She looked at Jeff. His eyes flashed, and glancing down she saw the sun glint silver on her shoes.

'You'd better come in for a cup of tea.'

Much, much later they went to bed. Joy lay across his hot body.

'Don't say nothing. Don't utter a word.' She stretched out her hand and put her fingers over his lips. 'Don't even open your mouth. Just pretend it's your birthday.'

A NOTE ON THE AUTHOR

Nell Dunn was born and still lives in London. Her first book, *Up the Junction*, published in 1963, was made into a TV film by Kenneth Loach, and won the John Llewellyn Rhys Memorial Prize. *Poor Cow*, her first novel, was also made into a film and directed by Kenneth Loach. Since then she has written many other books and plays, including the highly successful play and film *Steaming*, directed by Joseph Losey.